A Dog
Called
Kitty

BILL WALLACE

A Dog
Called
Kitty

Holiday House • New York

Library of Congress Cataloging in Publication Data

Wallace, Bill, 1947–
  A dog called Kitty.

  SUMMARY: Afraid of dogs since he was attacked by a
mad one, Ricky resists taking in a homeless pup that
shows up at the farm.
  [1. Dogs–Fiction] I. Title.
PZ7.W15473Do   [Fic]   80–16293
ISBN 0–8234–0376–9

to Laurie, Nikki and Justin

Chapter 1

I don't reckon there's any time as pretty as early in the morning. The time of day when the sun is up, but it hasn't been there long enough to chase the silvery dewdrops off the grass.

It's specially pretty in late spring. The birds are back from their nesting places in the south. All that chirping and fluttering in the trees makes a certain kind of music. Tells you winter's over, and it's time for things to start growing and turning green.

I guess I didn't notice that time of day when we lived in town. When you live in an apartment house in a big city like St. Louis, there aren't many birds and things to study on. There're a lot of car horns to listen to. If you look up in the sky, you can see smoke from some of the factories by the river. But there aren't many birds.

Probably the only thing that saved me from listening to car horns and breathing the funny smelling air that hangs over St. Louis like a thick brown cloud was Dad's dream.

Far back as I could remember, Dad was talking about a farm. About how he used to visit his grandparents in the country. And he had this dream about some day moving from the big city and getting a farm all his own.

Mama—she said he was just dreaming. When Dad would get to talking about it too much, she'd remind him of that fact. Always say something about how he didn't know the first thing about farming. How he couldn't leave a good job like he had and all sorts of stuff.

Then, lo and behold, we woke up one morning and found Dad wasn't dreaming anymore.

There was this big moving van parked in front of our apartment. When Mama said something about the neighbors upstairs must be leaving, Dad only smiled and went to open the front door. Mama got downright *upset* when the men started hauling her furniture away. That's when Dad showed her the deed to a house and 160 acres of land in Oklahoma.

Mama didn't do anything but stand and stare at him for a long, long time. Then, she got real pale and sickly looking. And when she commenced crying and laughing—both at the same time—that's when Dad told me and Chuckie to go outside and play. Even out there, we could hear the fussin' and arguin' that came from our place. All the other folks in our end of the apartment complex must have heard it, too. 'Cause they kept looking out their windows or coming out on the sidewalk to see what was going on. Mom and Dad went right on yelling and fussin' until the men from the moving company had everything hauled out and were waiting in their truck.

At last, Dad opened the front door and started down the steps. He stopped and looked back at Mama. Then, in a real soft voice, he said, "I love you more than you'll ever know, Helen. My life wouldn't be much without you." Then, his face got real stern looking. "But me and my sons are moving to that farm in Oklahoma. We want you to come. We need you with us. But, with or without you—I've made up my mind."

I don't remember being so scared about anything as when Dad said that. He marched me and Chuckie to the car. We got in the back, and he got in front. Started the engine.

I was about to cry. I told him I didn't want to go

any place without Mama—only he didn't answer me.

Chuckie didn't help me much. He was busy chewing on his toy car and picking his nose. I guess he didn't say anything 'cause he was too little to know how much trouble our family was in.

Dad put the car in gear. My heart almost jumped up in my throat when he started to drive away.

It was about then Mama came trotting out the front door. She had her purse on her arm. Jumping on one foot trying to pull on her shoes. Dad stopped the car. She got in.

But it was clean into the next day before Mama said one single word. Then it was only to tell Dad she needed to stop at a filling station to go to the bathroom.

Her mad spell lasted almost two weeks. We had moved into our new house and had things pretty well settled—everything except Mom and Dad, that is. Mama was still pouting. Not talking to Dad. She even slept in the bedroom with Chuckie at night.

Anyway, it was Chuckie who finally snapped her out of her orneriness. She was getting him ready for his bath one night, and I guess he'd finally noticed that things weren't running quite as smooth as they usually did. I was sitting in the living room watching TV with Dad when he came racing in.

He was stark-naked and red as a lobster from the

top of his head clean down to his bellybutton. (When he got mad, Chuckie held his breath until he was about to pop, but I don't ever remember him being as red as he was that night.)

Chuckie marched up in front of Dad. He squared off and kicked him right on the shins.

Dad sorta jumped, not quite knowing why Chuckie had kicked him, and not quite being able to figure out why he was naked as a jaybird and red all over.

Finally, Chuckie opened his mouth and let out all his air. Then, he scrunched his little round face up till he was real mean and angry looking.

"I don't know why Mommy's so mad at you. But I'm mad, too. My Daddy's a mean, mean old toot!"

I guess Dad had been real worried about Mama not liking our new home, and so upset about the way she'd been treating him lately, he was ready to pop.

And that's just what he did. He started laughing so hard the whole room seemed to shake. His belly bounced up and down and tears leaked from his eyes.

Mama had been watching from the door of Chuckie's bedroom. It wasn't any time before she was doubled over laughing, too. Directly, she came into the living room and sat down on Dad's lap.

All that laughing only made Chuckie mad. He stood there in front of them and turned red, all over.

That only made Mama and Dad laugh harder.

I didn't know what they were laughing so hard about but, after watching Chuckie for a while, I got to laughing, too.

Finally, Mama scooped Chuckie up in her arms and snuggled him up real tight. Dad waved for me to come over and sit on the arm of his chair. All four of us sat there, and Mama told us why she'd been so upset about leaving everything to move to a farm in Oklahoma. But she said she'd decided it wasn't such a bad place after all, that she was glad we were together and happy again, and that she wasn't mad at Dad anymore, and we shouldn't be, either.

All that happened more than two years ago. But even now as I remember it, I can't help chuckling to myself. I can't help thinking how lucky we are that Mama didn't stay back in St. Louis.

I guess I'd got so wrapped up in remembering how we came to live on our farm near Chickasha, Oklahoma, I plumb forgot about what was going on around me.

One of the cats from the barn came tearing past and brushed against my leg. It startled me so much, I almost fell down when I turned around to see what hit me.

Mama let the screen door slam behind her when she brought out a bowl of table scraps to feed the cats. The bowl made a clanking sound when she set it down on top of the old rock cellar. She turned and cupped her hand to her mouth.

"Here kitty, kitty," she called.

Her calling didn't do much good. The six scraggly old cats Dad kept around to run mice out of the barn were already coming on the run.

I was standing between Mama and the barn. When I saw them coming I stood real still, hoping they wouldn't trample me in their mad rush to get at their food.

Mama stepped away from the bowl. Shook her head.

"Think those fool cats hadn't eaten in a week." She glanced up at me. "Didn't you feed them last night?"

"Yes, mam," I answered. "There was a whole bowl full of scraps. And I fed them some of that dry food, too."

Mama shook her head. Smiled.

"I hope they act this hungry when they're chasing mice out of your father's grain bin."

Suddenly, I caught a movement from the corner of my eye. Something brown and fuzzy. Whatever it was, though, disappeared under the car before I could see it.

Frowning, I aimed down my finger at the cats. Sure enough, all six of them were clamoring around the feed bowl. I didn't remember Dad saying anything about us getting another cat either. So, I put my hand on the back of the car for a brace and leaned way down to see what was there.

That's when it came trotting out.

I was so close to the ground that its floppy, droopy tail almost slapped me upside the head. It was interested in the food, and it didn't bother to glance up. I jumped away. Bumped my side against the fender of the car and almost tore my hip out of socket.

Before I knew what was happening, I was sitting on top of the car looking down.

The fuzzy thing I saw going under the car was a dog. Well . . . not really a dog—'cause it was too little and clumsy to be a full-fledged dog. It was a puppy.

Its coat was brown and the long, scraggly hair was covered with mud and dirt.

Watching from the top of the car, I unconsciously rubbed a finger over the scars below my right eye. The other hand rubbed at the long, rough mark on the back of my neck. It wasn't until I'd rubbed long and hard so the scars started stinging that I realized what I was doing.

About then Mama spotted the pup. She smiled, then turned to where I was. Her face got real serious and scared looking. Then, she tried to smile again.

"It's all right, Ricky," she consoled. "It's just a little old pup. He won't bother you."

A trembling shot up my back. A shaking that started in my legs and ended in the bristly hair at the back of my neck. A quivering that I couldn't stop, no matter how hard I tried.

Mama must have noticed the way I was acting. She flipped her skirt at the pup.

"Get!" she yelled. "Get on outa here."

Only the mangy-looking brown pup didn't pay her any mind. He just trotted over to the feed bowl and muscled his way in alongside our cats.

I reckon at first they figured he was one of them. But when they found out he was a dog, you never heard such a commotion in your life.

They jumped back, trying to get away from him. In about as long as it takes a mosquito to blink its eyes, they got fuzzed up all over, their tails puffed out as big as they were.

The old tom kinda stepped back and must have decided the dog wasn't as big as it first looked. He inched his way toward the feed bowl. Real careful like, he scooted up next to the pup.

The dog was so busy stealing the table scraps, he didn't know he was being snuck up on. Not until it was too late, anyways.

All of a sudden, the old cat flicked out a paw. It

caught the pup right across his soft nose and sent him reeling back on his haunches.

When the cats saw him run back, they set in after him.

I never heard such spitting and squalling in my life. There was suddenly a pile of furry cats, all squealing and scratching and pouncing on that one pup.

The "fight" only lasted about a second. 'Cause, soon as there was a break in the circle of cats, the pup lit out for wherever he came from. Tail tucked between his legs, he went whining and squealing. At a deadout run, he shot under the car and came tearing out on the other side.

The tomcat chased him for a ways. But when he noticed the others had gone back to eating, he gave up the chase so he wouldn't miss out on the food.

That pup didn't know he wasn't being chased anymore. He kept right on running. Squealing and whining like he'd almost been killed. The last I saw of him, he was running scared around behind the hay barn with his tail tucked under him.

Things were over about as quick as they started. The cats settled back to their meal. Mama stood by the door and shook her head.

"Poor little thing didn't stand a chance," she commented. Then to me, "Ricky, I'm about ready. You need anything from inside?"

I climbed off the car, feeling things were safe, now. "No, mam. I'm ready."

She went back after her purse and keys, and I got into the car to wait.

Seemed like ever since we moved to the farm, that's what I spent my time doing—waiting.

I waited on the school bus in the mornings. I waited for the wind to stop blowing so I could go fishing. I waited for my horse, Beauty, to come in from the pasture so I could catch her and go riding. I waited for Brad McNeil to have his parents bring him out to visit. I waited for Mama to drive me into town so I could play football with the guys, like I was gonna do today.

I'd been waiting on that since early this morning.

Finally, she was ready to go. She came out and got in the car.

Chapter 2

Mama let me off in front of the high school football stadium. That's where the boys from my school were playing football this morning.

Brad McNeil, my best friend, had told me about the hole in the fence at the west side of the stadium. He said that nobody came around to check on Saturdays, and it was probably all right for us to play.

I didn't tell Mama that. But I said that Brad told me everybody played there, and that it was all right. I really didn't lie to her—I just forgot to tell her we were sneaking under the fence to get in.

"Are you sure anyone's here?" she asked as I started to get out. "I don't see any of the gates open."

I nodded, remembering the bicycles parked beside the stadium as we drove up.

"They're here," I answered. "I figure one of the gates on the other side is open."

Mama kinda raised her eyebrows.

"I suppose it's all right," she said with a shrug. "I'll be back after I do some shopping. Take about two hours or so."

"That'll be fine," I answered, closing the door. "Just honk the horn. I'll be listening."

I walked toward the front of the stadium real slow until Mama turned the corner at the end of the street. Then I took off around the side where I'd seen the bicycles parked.

Sure enough, Brad had told me right.

There, by the fifth evergreen bush, was a little dirt path. I got down on my knees and followed it through the bushes. And just beyond was the hole in the stadium fence he'd told me about.

The guys were down at the other end of the field, beyond the water sprinklers. I shot through the spray, just as they swung apart, and joined Brad without getting a drop on me.

Charlie Jenks and Ben Parlen started clapping and yelling when Brad and I marched down the field. Only, I figured they weren't all excited about me being on their team. It was just that Sammy Darlinger had one more guy on his side than Brad did, and they were glad I was there so the teams would be even.

Charlie and Ben slapped me on the back as we huddled up. Brad called the play. All he said was, "Run for the goal line when you get open, and I'll hit you."

Charlie snapped the ball, and we took off. Sammy Darlinger was covering me, only, when he figured out it was a pass play, he left off and went toward Ben. Guess he figured there was no way I could catch the ball, and Ben was pretty good at it.

Right then, Brad spotted me open. When I saw him draw back, I was kinda wishing he wouldn't throw it at me, 'cause I'd probably drop it.

Just like I was afraid of, when Brad saw me behind the goal line, he threw it right at me.

I guess he was excited 'cause he threw it harder than usual. The thing smacked me right in the stomach. When it did, I slapped my arms shut around it.

The nose of that pointed, little ball sure hurt. I closed my eyes when it hit. But when I opened my eyes, danged if that ball wasn't sitting there in my arms.

It must have surprised Brad more than it did me. He flung his arms straight up over his head.

"Touchdown," he yelled. Then he started jumping

up and down. Dancing around all over the place.

I just started back toward him to tell him what a great pass it was, when somebody slammed into me from behind.

I wasn't expecting it, 'cause I figured the play was already over. Whoever it was hit me with his head, square in the back. Hit so hard that the ball went flying out of my hands, and I pitched forward, landing on the ground and getting a mouthful of dirt.

The tackle knocked the air out of me for a second. When I finally got up, Sammy Darlinger had the football.

"No touchdown," he laughed. "Ricky fumbled the ball, and we recovered."

I got up and dusted myself off. Brad came walking over to help me.

"That's cheating, Sammy. The play was already over. You tackled Ricky after he'd caught the ball and was walking back."

"Did not," Sammy sneered. "If he can't hang onto it when he gets tackled, it's a fumble. No touchdown."

"Is, too," Ben and Charlie came running over. "We saw it, Sammy. The play was over. You didn't get close to Ricky until he'd done caught the ball and started walking out of the end zone. Touchdown counts."

Larry Allen and Paul Sparks, two of the guys on Sammy's team, came walking up.

"That's right," Larry said. "You tackled him too late, Sammy. They got a touchdown. Now, come on."

We were walking back toward the field when, all of a sudden, I felt somebody's hands on my back. I started to turn around, when he pushed—real hard.

It caught me off balance. And, before I could stop, I was heading straight for the sprinklers.

The grass was wet and slippery. First thing I knew, I was tumbling head over heels into the water.

I could feel myself slipping and sliding, only there wasn't anything I could do. Finally, my shoulder bumped against one of the pipes, and I stopped.

Quick as I could, I scrambled to my feet and ran out from under the spray. Only it didn't do any good. I was soaked. My tennis shoes made a sloshing sound when I walked. And I was so sopping wet that I could feel my underpants sticking to me.

Sammy was laughing his head off.

That made me mad.

I walked up close to him and shook some water off my head.

"What'd you go and do that for?"

He just laughed and sneered at me.

"I felt like it. That's why. You wanta do somethin' about it?"

Brad came trotting back to where we were.

"Man, Ricky," he gasped. "Your mom's gonna skin you alive when she sees this."

I looked down and saw the mud. It was all over one side. Clean from my shoulder to my shoes. It was gooey and black and sticky. Brad tried to clean off some of it. Only, the more we rubbed at it, the more it spread.

Sammy just kept on laughing.

"It's not funny," I said, finally. "These are the best pair of blue jeans I got. And Mama's gonna kill me when she sees this sweat shirt."

I was trying to get him to stop laughing. Only he just laughed harder when I said that. Then he got that squinty-eyed look on his face.

"You want to do something about it?" he growled.

"Leave him alone," Brad snapped.

"Get lost," Sammy sneered at him. He clenched his fists at his side. Moved toward me.

"Well, Ricky. You gonna fight me about it?"

I looked at him. I was the one who ought to be mad, not Sammy. But he just kept moving closer. Glaring at me with his tight eyes, like they were gonna cut clean through me.

I didn't know what to do. I knew I'd be in enough trouble at home for getting wet and muddy. If I got to fighting, Mama would switch me for sure. Then, again, all the guys were watching. I couldn't just turn tail and run from Sammy, either.

He walked right up in front of me and shoved me with one hand.

"You gonna fight me?"

I didn't answer. Sammy pushed again.

"What's wrong? Chicken?"

"Quit, Sammy."

"Make me," he sneered. Then, he pushed again.

"Sammy, I mean it. Let's just forget it. Let's go play."

I tried to turn away from him. Only, Sammy grabbed my arm and spun me around. Then, he socked me on the shoulder.

It was right then that something snapped inside me.

My head wasn't working very well, I guess. 'Cause I don't remember too much of what happened— there at first.

I do remember thinking, "I don't care if Dad busts the paddle in half over my seat. I'm not gonna take no more off Sammy."

It took me half a second to tear into him with everything I had. I must have gone out of my head. I don't remember what happened. Only I started swinging and hitting and wrestling Sammy all over the place.

When my wits finally came back, we were both under the water sprinklers. I was sitting on top of Sammy with both knees pinning his shoulders down.

And I was pounding him in the face with my fists as hard as I could hit.

Then I noticed he was so beat to a pulp, he was hardly fighting back. He was laying there on his back crying. Yelling at me.

"Don't hit me no more. Don't hit me."

I had my fist drawn back, ready to sock him again —when I caught hold of myself.

All of a sudden, I heard it.

Eyes wide, I looked around.

Sammy's Doberman was there beside us. He was barking and bouncing around, trying to find out what his master was yelling about.

Like a bolt of lightning, the old fear took hold of me.

Before I knew what was happening, I was in a panic. On my feet. Running. Running hard as I could.

Behind me, I heard Sammy yelling, "Get him, Butch. Sick him, boy. Tear his leg off."

The dog was barking. Right at my heels.

I knew it was going to happen again. Just like it had

before. I could almost feel his sharp teeth closing on my leg.

I knew if he bit me, I'd fall. I'd be there on the ground. Helpless. I'd be laying there, and that dog would be tearing me to shreds.

Chapter 3

How I got on top of the fence behind the bleachers, I still don't know. Like I said, I was in a panic and didn't know what I was doing.

Anyhow, that's where Brad finally found me. I was balanced clean on the top of the fence, and Sammy's dog was bouncing around barking his head off.

Brad came running. He acted like he was picking up a rock. When Sammy's dog saw him, he tucked in his stub tail and lit out for the bushes.

Brad shook his head.

"That dog's just like Sammy. He makes a lot of noise but he's a coward at heart."

Then, he looked up at me.

"You had Sammy beat to a pulp. That dog wasn't gonna hurt you. How come you took off running like that?"

I was shaking so hard, I couldn't answer. I knew I was crying, too. I could feel the warm, wet tears on my cheeks. I didn't want Brad to see me cry, only there wasn't much I could do about it.

"The dog's gone. Come on down."

I hesitated. Looked around to make sure Sammy's dog wasn't hiding some place.

Brad waved again.

"Come on, Ricky. You're gonna fall off that fence and break your fool neck."

I pointed at the field.

"Why don't you go back to the football game," I sniffed. "Go on. Leave me alone."

Brad frowned.

"The game's over. Sammy went home, and some men came to move the sprinkler pipes and told us to stay off the field." He looked up and shook his head. "Now come on down from there or I'll shake you off. I'm gonna find out what's wrong with you."

It finally came to me that Brad was as bullheaded as I was. The only way to make him leave me alone was to tell him the whole story, much as I hated to talk about it.

"All right!"

He helped me off the fence. We walked around to the side of the cement bleachers at the stadium. Waited there until the men were finished moving the sprinklers.

When they were gone, we walked to the top of the bleachers.

From up there, you could see real far. We leaned over the edge and spit a couple of times. Watched the wind whip it round and round until it disappeared out of sight before it hit the ground.

We looked down on the park for a long time. Pointed out different things to each other. And spit a few more times from the top of the stadium. Finally, Brad nudged me with his elbow.

"You said you'd tell me what happened," he reminded me.

I pretended I didn't hear him. Only he just punched me with his elbow again.

"Ricky. If you tell me, maybe I can help."

I turned around and sat down on the top step. Brad sat beside me. I bit at my lip. Folded my hands between my knees.

"It happened a long time ago," I began. "I don't really remember. Mostly, I remember 'cause Mama and Dad told me about it. I wasn't even as old as little Chuckie is. Not even old enough to remember good, I guess. Anyhow, I was playing in the yard near our apartment one day when this big dog came trotting by. I was just a little kid, like I said, and I didn't know any better. So when he came running past me, I reached out and tried to pet him. He tore into me like I was his worst enemy. It's kinda funny . . ." I stopped, gazing off into the clear Oklahoma sky. ". . . only, I don't remember him biting me. I got this scar, here under my right eye." I pointed it out to Brad. "And there're places on my arms and my back where he bit me . . . only . . . well . . . I don't remember that part of it at all. It's almost like it didn't really happen."

I closed my eyes. Shuddered as I remembered other things.

"The first thing I recollect was this man came along and got the dog off me. He was yelling and screaming at it. Finally, he grabbed it by the neck and locked it in the pump house beside the swimming pool. Then, he came back and picked me up.

"He thought I was dead, 'cause I heard him call to his wife that the dog had killed me. Then, I guess he figured I was alive. He picked me up and said something about how I was gonna bleed to death.

"That's about when Mama came running out of our apartment. She saw me and went to crying and screaming. I guess that scared me, 'cause I went to crying and screaming, too. I remember them taking me to the hospital. The doctor got this long, curved needle and started sewing me up."

I couldn't help biting down on my lip as I remembered that part.

"It hurt worse than the dog biting me," I confessed. "I screamed and cried and begged Mama to make him quit. But he didn't until I had about sixty-three stitches in me.

"Two days later, we had to go back to the hospital. The police came and got the dog out of where the man had locked him in the pump house. They told Mama and Dad that he was 'mad.' Had a disease called hydrophobia. The doctors said I'd have to take a bunch of shots to keep from getting the sickness and dying."

I felt the tears going down my cheeks when I told Brad that part. But no matter how hard I tried, I couldn't stop them.

"Those shots were the worst thing of all," I said. "They hurt worse than the dog bites and the stitches put together. I screamed and kicked when I first saw the needle. It looked as long as my whole arm. Two doctors held me down and the other one gave me the shot, right into my stomach.

"When he put the stuff in me, it was like my whole stomach was on fire. I screamed until my ears almost busted. Only the burning wouldn't stop. It just kept hurting 'till I thought sure I was gonna die. Two days later, we had to go back for another shot. Then again, two days after that. I lost count of how many times we went back. Mama said it was twelve shots I took. But I remember the hurting. I remember those doctors holding me down, and I remember screaming and feeling like I was burning all over, and I remember . . ."

I had to stop talking, then. I was rubbing at my stomach. And I couldn't stand talking about it anymore, 'cause I was crying and remembering it, just like it was happening all over again.

Brad must have understood how I felt. He didn't say anything to me for a long time. He didn't even look at me.

Finally, I heard him let out a long sigh.

"That's awful bad, Ricky. I can understand how come you had to run when Sammy's dog came running up. I . . . I reckon I'd be scared of dogs, too, if something bad as that happened to me."

We still weren't looking at each other. Brad sat with his head down, kinda looking at his tennis shoes. We were quiet for a long time, then he said, "I guess everybody's afraid of one thing or another. Me, I'm afraid of spiders. Only I don't have a good reason to be, like you got to be scared of dogs."

I looked up at my friend. He frowned and

scratched at his chin. All of a sudden, his face lit up.

"Hey, I got a great idea! Why don't I find my dog, Ruff. He's real gentle. Never bit anybody in his life. Maybe, with me helping, you could get used to being around him. Might even get where you could pet him."

"No," I snapped, cutting him off.

"But, Ricky . . . it wouldn't hurt to try."

"No!"

"Why not? You can't spend the rest of your life running every time you see a dog. It's not natural."

"I said no, Brad," I yelled at him.

"Come on, Ricky. Just try."

"No!"

"But . . ."

"No. I said no, and I mean it. I don't want anything to do with any old stinking dog."

"You know Sammy's gonna tell the guys what happened today. If you don't get over being scared of dogs by the end of summer, everybody in school's gonna pester you next year."

"I don't care."

"But, Ricky . . ."

"No, Brad! Just forget it!"

"Listen, Ricky . . ."

I reckon Brad and I woulda gone on arguing about it for the rest of the day. Only about then we heard a horn honking from the other side of the stadium.

We knew it was Mama, so Brad and I hurried down from the bleachers and went out through the hole in the fence.

I was halfway scared to let Mama see me with my good clothes muddy and messed up—only there wasn't much I could do but go to the car.

Brad was my best friend. I always knew that. But I didn't know how good he was until he went to the car and explained to Mama what happened.

He told her how I couldn't help fighting with Sammy. And how it wasn't my fault. He even tried to take some of the blame for not running Sammy off when the bully first started acting up.

Mama listened to him. And after he was through, she wasn't mad at me anymore. She even invited Brad to come spend Saturday with me. She said she'd call his mother tonight and see if it was all right.

I was so excited about Brad getting to come out, I didn't think about anything else all the way home. I forgot about fighting with Sammy. I forgot about dogs. I even forgot about my clothes being muddy, and what Dad might say if he saw I'd been fighting.

Mama didn't forget, though. She stopped at the mailbox down the hill from our house. After she got the mail from the tin box, she turned to me.

"Soon as we get to the house, you scoot inside and

put on some old clothes. Your dad finds out you been fighting . . . well, I just think it'd be best if you change before you go help with the chores."

It was a good idea—only things didn't work out like Mama and me planned. When she stopped in front of the house, I jumped out and headed for the back door. Dad was usually down at the barn this time of day. But just as I hit the back screen, he came out the door. I smacked square into him, mud and all.

Right then, I could tell I was in trouble. He didn't say anything, but I knew by the look on his face.

Real quick, I jumped back. Sorta turned sideways, trying to hide the muddiest side of me. Only it was too late. He looked me over. Up and down. Then he sorta sighed, and his eyes got real sad looking.

Without a word, he walked on toward the barn.

I knew he was mad. And when I saw Mama trailing after him, I hoped maybe she could make him understand what happened.

Boy, was I ever wrong.

Chapter 4

By the time I got my clothes changed and started downstairs from my room, I wasn't so worried about Dad being mad at me. There wasn't anything for me to be ashamed of. After all, it wasn't my fault that Sammy Darlinger was a bully. It wasn't my fault he picked a fight with me. Dad was sure to understand.

Mama met me in the kitchen. Right off, I could tell she was worried about something.

"Your dad wants you to stack that load of oat straw he bought day before yesterday," she said. "It's up in the barn." She paused. Glanced out the kitchen window. "Your dad went down by the stock pens. Maybe if you work real hard and steer clear of him, he'll cool down by suppertime."

"Cool down?" I yelped. "You don't mean he's mad about me fighting?"

She nodded her head.

"You know your father doesn't take to fighting. You'll have to be patient with him. Try to understand how he feels."

"Understand how *he* feels," I yelped. "Why can't he understand how *I* feel. That fight wasn't my fault. He ought to be proud of me for taking up for myself."

Mama sighed and looked away.

"Just go on and do your chores," she said. "And if your father comes up to talk to you, don't argue with him. Understand?"

I didn't answer. For some reason, I was mad as all get out. So, I just stormed off. Up the hill toward the hay barn.

The oat straw was piled in the corner of the barn. Most of the time, when Dad bought hay, he'd have the men who brought it throw it into the barn without stacking it. Then, to save money, we'd do the stacking.

The big bales of alfalfa hay were too heavy for me to tote around, so Dad stacked them. But the brown bales of oat straw or wheat hay were light. Since I could handle those without too much trouble, stacking oat straw was one of my big chores around the place.

When I saw the way those men had thrown the hay into the barn, I decided it was a bigger chore than I'd planned on.

There were about fifty bales of oat straw jumbled and thrown on top of one another. The messy pile was right in front of the door, and I had to climb over it. To make matters worse, the stuff was down at the end of the barn where Dad stacked the alfalfa. That meant I'd have to drag each bale clear to the other end of the big barn so it wouldn't get mixed in with the alfalfa.

If I hadn't been so mad, I might have gone to ask Dad if he'd help me. But as it was, I grabbed hold and started to work by myself. The more I thought about Dad not understanding, the madder I got. And, the madder I got, the harder I worked.

By the time Mama called supper, I only had five bales of hay left to stack. I trotted to the door and cupped my hand to my mouth.

"I'll be there in just a second," I shouted. "I'm almost through."

I could see Mama at the back door. She nodded her head real big and waved, showing me that she'd heard.

The barn was partly dark inside. The last few bales were over in a corner. I grabbed hold of the wire on one and started dragging it toward the stack. When I did, I thought I heard a sound from behind one of the other bales.

I froze. Stood real still, listening. But when the sound didn't come again, I decided it was only my imagination and went on about what I was doing.

When I got hold of another bale, I heard the sound again. This time, I was sure it wasn't just my imagination. Real careful, I leaned over and pulled another bale out of the way. Then another, trying to see what it was I heard.

The last bale was leaning up against the corner. I tipped it over—and that's when I saw him.

It was the pup.

I'd forgotten about him coming down with our cats this morning. When I saw him hiding under the hay bale, it scared me.

I jumped so hard, my head hit the side of the barn. Tin rattled all over the place. And so did my head.

The little pup just lay there for a second. He tilted his head to the side and cocked his floppy ears, like he was trying to figure what I was.

Then, 'fore I knew what was happening, his face sorta lit up. All of a sudden, he was on his feet. His tail was wagging so hard that it shook his whole back end.

He yapped a couple of times, then started toward me.

Like always, the old fear took hold. I backed away from him. He only came toward me faster.

In a flash, I turned and started running. When I did that, the pup took in after me. He kept wagging and yapping. Chased me all over the barn.

I tried to get out the door once. But he got there before I did.

Finally, I got away from him by climbing up the bales of hay that I'd just stacked. He couldn't follow me up the bales. But he stood there at the bottom. He'd bounce around, wiggling all over the place. Then, he'd stop and yap at me.

"Get," I screamed. "Get away from me! Leave me alone!"

He tilted his head to the side and cocked his ears, giving me that dumb look again. His teeth weren't very big, least they didn't seem like it from up top of the haystack, but his tongue kinda flopped out the side of his mouth. It was probably long enough to drag the ground. And I was sure with all the jumping around he was doing, he was bound to trip over it. Only he never did.

I don't know how long he kept me up there. Mama

called dinner again. I was scared to yell for help. As it was, I was in enough trouble with Dad and, if he had to come up and rescue me from this little pup, I knew sure he'd be mad as blazes.

I didn't know what to do.

"Get," I screamed again. I raised my fist. Shook it at him. "Get, or I'll beat your head off."

He just lolled that long, sticky tongue out and cocked his ears again.

Next, I got my feet behind one of the hay bales and rolled it off the stack. It hit with a thud. Dust and old dry hay belched up around it.

For a second, I felt sorta bad, figuring I'd squashed the stuffing out of him.

But when the dust cleared, there he was. He was still bouncing around, wagging that bushy tail.

When I rolled a second bale off at him, he started yapping again. Acted like it was a game or something.

I felt ashamed of myself. The pup wasn't much bigger than a cottontail rabbit, and I reckon he was about as vicious, too. Only being scared of dogs like I was, I was scared to come down. Even if he was little and scrawny, he was still a dog. And I had good reason to be scared of dogs.

He could have kept me up there for the rest of the night if it hadn't been for Mama.

About the time I was fixin' to yell for help, I heard her open the back screen down at the house. She rattled the pans together and yelled, "Here, kitty, kitty, kitty."

The pup stopped looking at me and turned toward the door of the barn. When Mama called the cats again, he lit out for the house like somebody'd set his shaggy tail on fire with a match.

I waited for a second, then climbed off the hay-stack. At the door of the barn, I looked to make sure he was headed for the house. Then I lit out in a big circle so I could come up in front of the house instead of in the back where the dog was.

Just about the time I got to the front door, that pup must have got to the feed bowl where the cats were eating. You never heard such a commotion in your life.

Even from the other side of the house, I could hear the cats squalling and spitting. The pup yapped a couple of times, then yelped real good. He kept right on yelping as his voice trailed off toward the barn. I felt proud of the cats for running him off again.

Mama and Dad were standing by the back screen, watching. I scooted into my place at the table and waited, like I'd been there all along.

Mama shook her head. Turned back toward the table.

"Poor little thing. He'll starve if those cats don't let him eat with them."

Dad nodded.

"Somebody probably dumped him up the road, and he wandered here. Hard tellin' how long he's been without food. If it wasn't for Ricky being afraid of dogs, I'd . . ."

He stopped suddenly when he saw me sitting at the table.

"Where'd you come from?"

I shrugged and kinda smiled.

"Came in the front. This sure looks good, Mama," I said, trying to change the subject. "What is it?"

"Tuna casserole," she answered. She sat down in her chair beside me. "You usually don't like it."

I gave a half-grin and shrugged.

"Guess I'm extra hungry today. Stacking hay's hard work."

We all started eating then. I didn't much like tuna casserole but, the way things had been going, I didn't dare complain. Dad and Mama visited some about going to town and the weather. I figured maybe Dad had forgot about my fight. And I ate all hunkered down in my chair, trying not to bring anybody's attention to me.

Chuckie was the one who messed things up, though. Everybody was busy talking and eating. Nobody asked me anything, and I just pretended I wasn't there.

Right about then, Chuckie gave me that "little brother" sneer. That look that says "I'm gonna get you."

"Look what Ricky got on his foot, Mama."

"What?" she asked, not really paying much attention.

"Ricky stepped in the cow stuff," he announced.

I glanced down at my foot. Sure enough, I guess I'd been in such a hurry getting away from the pup, I didn't notice where I was stepping. Along with being on my shoe, there were big, green spots trailing through the living room to the front door.

Mama leaned around to where she could see what I was looking at.

"Oh, Ricky." She sighed. "And I just swept that carpet this morning."

"I'm sorry. I didn't . . ."

"You get outside, right now," she said. "Go get that off your feet."

I eased up from the table. Chuckie sneered again. Then, sure nobody was looking except me, he stuck his tongue out.

One of these days, I thought, I'm gonna tie a knot in that tongue of his. Now wasn't the time, though. I was in enough trouble as it was. Besides, if I so much as looked mean at him, he'd yell and I'd catch it.

Without a word, I went on outside like Mama said.

Just as I feared, Dad started asking me about the fight when I got back. I told him as best I could that it wasn't my fault. Only that didn't seem to make him any happier.

He made me tell every bit of it. Even though I didn't want to, I knew by looking at him he was in no mood for me to fool around and not answer.

"How did it end?" he asked.

I kinda bit down on my lip.

"Well, I was whoppin' him good and . . . and . . . and . . ."

"And," he snapped. "Go on."

"And then Sammy's dog came running up and started barking at us. I got scared and ran."

"Where to?"

" 'Round back of the stadium. I climbed up on the fence."

Dad looked away. Shook his head.

I slammed my fork down in my plate.

"I couldn't help it," I said. "I can't help being scared of dogs. And I couldn't help getting in that fight, either. It wasn't my idea."

Dad whirled around in his chair.

"I'm not worried about the fight," he snapped. He

blew a short blast of air up his forehead. Held his breath, like he was trying to calm himself. "Sometimes a man has to stand up for what he thinks is right. Fightin' never solved anything, never does anybody any good, but it happens sometimes. I can understand that. What I *can't* understand is why you act like a blamed idiot every time you get near a dog."

I glared across the table at him.

"What'd you want me to do? Stay there and get chewed up, like when I was little?"

I was shaking all over. Worse than that, I could feel the tears welling up in my eyes. I was mad at Dad for gettin' onto me for something I couldn't help.

"Now don't start that danged bawlin'," he barked. "You're gettin' too big for that foolishness. You're not a little baby anymore, Rick. It's time you started growin' up. Started takin' on some responsibility."

Mama reached over and touched Dad lightly on the arm.

"Now, honey. Don't be too hard on him. You know he can't help how he is about dogs. After what happened to him when he was a baby, I don't blame him a . . ."

"That was a long time ago," Dad cut her off. Then he turned back to me. "You can't let something that happened that long back keep gnawing at you, son."

With Dad yelling and Mom taking up for me, I felt

like I was trapped in the middle. A single tear rolled down my cheek, and I tried to wipe it away before Dad could see.

"I can't help being scared of dogs." I sniffed. "I just can't help it."

Dad shook his head.

"It's one thing to be scared of something. But you can't let fear run your life. You can't let it stampede you, make you do crazy things that you can't even remember. It's something you got to overcome. Fear is something you got to control. Somethin' you got to beat before it beats you."

"What do you want me to do?" I yelled. "You're always pickin' at me, but you never tell me what you want me to do!"

The knots in my stomach were so tight, I was shaking all over.

"Ricky," Mama scolded. "Don't talk to your father in that tone of voice."

I didn't realize I was almost screaming until Mama stopped me.

Dad's eyes got real tight. I bit down on my lip. Wished I hadn't lost my temper and yelled like I did.

I figured any second Dad'd stand up from his chair and start taking his belt off. And I reckon I deserved it, too. Only he just sat there. His voice was real calm when he said, "Go up to your room. Now."

Chapter 5

It was almost bedtime before anyone came up to see me. Mama sent Chuckie in to get his pajamas. And while he was messin' around in the bathroom, she sat down on the edge of my bed.

"I'm sorry," she said, patting my forehead. "Your father really tries to understand how you feel about dogs . . . but . . . well, he just can't."

She sighed and looked out the window.

I was looking out the window, too. Not that there was anything new to see. It was 'cause I was feeling kinda ashamed of myself, and I didn't want to look her square in the eye.

"I know I shouldn't have sassed him," I admitted.

"But it isn't really my fault. I can't help being scared around dogs. He ought to understand about that. He ought to know how I feel. I bet if he'd been chewed on by a dog when he was little, he'd understand."

Mama acted like she was wanting to say something. Only she changed her mind.

We sat quiet for a time. Finally, she eased up from the bed.

"I better go check on Chuckie. He's probably got water running over the top of the bathtub by now."

At the door, she paused and looked back at me.

"I don't think your father's mad at you. He's a little hurt, that's all. I think it hurt his feelings to know his son would talk to him like you did."

I bit down on my bottom lip.

"I know I shouldn't have done it Mama. I'm sorry. It's only . . . well . . ."

She gave a knowing smile.

"I understand. I think your father does, too. Still, he *is* right. Fear is something you got to overcome. You can't let it run your life. There're too many dogs in this world for you to run from. If you keep running, you'll be so busy running, there won't be time for anything else."

I looked up at her. I wanted to say something, argue with her, or say I was sorry again. Only I just lay there and watched her leave.

Leaving me alone in my room was about the worst kind of punishment. Being alone, I had plenty of time to think. When you're right, the thinking isn't too bad. But when you know your Dad and Mama are right and you're wrong—well, thinking that over is awful painful.

Sleep didn't come quick that night. I did a lot of tossin' and turnin' and could never quite get comfortable.

Morning came awful early, too.

I felt like I'd barely gotten to sleep when this terrible squealing and yelping and hissing yanked me awake. I blinked a couple of times and sat up. The noise was coming from right under my window. Still half asleep, I stumbled over to see what was going on.

Down below, out in the backyard, our six cats were all fuzzed up and squalling at that floppy-eared pup again. Fur and hair were flying every place and, there was so much noise, a dead person couldn't have slept through it.

Out of the corner of my eye, I saw Mama run out. She commenced swatting the cats with her broom and yelling at them. I reckon she was figuring on rescuing that pup.

They all scattered when she flopped them. And when the pup saw the broom, he lit out, too. Mama called after him. Tried to coax him back to the bowl she'd brought out just for him.

Only that pup was having no more of it. He went whining with his tail tucked between his legs. Once he looked back to see if anyone was chasing him. When he did, he stumbled over a dirt clod and went tumbling head over heels.

From the look on his face when he got up, you'd have thought somebody chunked that clod at him. He yelped again and disappeared behind the barn.

The cats didn't waste any time getting back to their feed. Mama kinda raised the broom like she wanted to take another swat at them. She didn't, though.

I heard the screen door slam. In a few seconds, Dad came far enough into the yard that I could see him from my upstairs window.

"I thought I saw that pup up at the barn the other day," he said. "But when I went in there to run him out, I couldn't find him."

Mama nodded.

"He started trying to get the cat food about four days ago," she said. "I don't reckon he'll stay much longer. Those thieving cats haven't let him eat a bite since he got here."

Dad put his hands on his hips. Even from way down there, I could hear him sigh.

"That must be one tough little pup. At least four

days without food—it's a wonder he can still get around." He shook his head. "Shame people abandon a cute little pup like that. Down right shame."

"I don't understand why folks in town bring dogs out to the country and dump them," Mama said. "It'd be kinder to take them to the pound. Kinder to hit them over the head with a club than to let them starve to death."

Dad nodded.

"Yeah. It's really getting to be a problem. Bill Priddle, over by Lake Burtschi, told me the other day that a pack of dogs got one of his newborn calves. Said he trailed about seven of them until they got into the blackjack trees by the lake. Big dogs, too, he said."

Mama shook her head.

"It doesn't surprise me. I've driven that road before and seen up to ten dogs. They were just strays somebody had dumped. They weren't running in a pack, though."

Dad motioned to the barn.

"Won't have to worry about that little thing running with a pack," he sighed. "Fact is, much longer without food, we won't have to worry about him at all."

Dad and Mama went back inside. I looked toward the barn where the pup had disappeared.

It was a pleasant surprise to see Beauty standing there by the salt block. For over two weeks, my horse hadn't come near the house. She was a pretty good mare, gentle and all, but, when it came to catching her in an open pasture, she could run me to death, and I'd still have to walk back to the house.

Now was the perfect chance. If I could get dressed and close the corral gate before she left the salt block, I'd have her trapped.

I guess Beauty was as ready to go riding as I was. When I came around the side of the barn and headed for the gate, she didn't even try to outrun me and get away. She only stood there, swooshing her white tail.

Once I had her locked in the small corral, catching her was no problem. Within ten minutes, I had the bridle and saddle on, and we were headed for a whole day of fun.

Riding Beauty was just the thing I needed after the trouble with Dad last night. First off, we rode over on Mr. Shaw's place and explored the canyon below the big pond, where there are some tall oak trees with opossum grapevines hanging down. I tied Beauty up and climbed and swung on them a while.

Then, before lunch, we came back on our place and herded the cows a while. That didn't last long. When Dad drove by in the truck, he caught us.

"You two quit chasin' my cows," he called. "Gonna run all the fat off them."

At lunch, there was nothing said about the cows. Nothing said about last night, either. Maybe it was forgotten.

After I finished eating, I rode to the big rock hill northeast of our house. There was plenty of exploring to do there—paths and trails the cows used, plumb thickets and red-rock boulders to circle and hide behind.

It was almost dark when we came in. I took Beauty down to the barn where Dad was. He told me it would be all right to keep her in the calf pen tonight, so I could go riding again tomorrow.

The oats were stored in the grain bin inside the hay barn. After I took the bridle off Beauty and made sure she got a drink, I grabbed one of the cow feed buckets and lit out for the barn.

All in all, it had been a beautiful day. Maybe all the troubles were over for a while.

But, sure enough, the trouble started again when Mama rattled the pans down at the house and yelled, "Here kitty, kitty, kitty."

I clean forgot about the stray pup who'd been fighting our cats.

But when Mama yelled, I remembered him right quick.

I was digging into the grain bin for the oats when all of a sudden, I heard this whining sound right beside me. It was kinda weak and far off. Then, the next second, I heard a bark and another whine.

The sound of a dog sent the chills running through me. Without thinking, I dropped the bucket, slammed the lid of the grain bin, and crawled up on top of it.

The whining sound came again. And I figured the pup was down beside the bin some place. Only, from up on top of the box like I was, I couldn't see him.

Any minute, I figured to see him running for the house. Only, the barking and jumping around he did this morning never came.

He whimpered some more, more like a little baby crying than a dog yelping. It was a soft sound. Far off, yet coming from some grain sacks right beside me. Then the whimpering stopped. Things got so quiet, I could hear my stomach growling.

There was a pitchfork hanging above the grain bin. I took it down. Reckon I was planning to take care of that pup, once and for all, if he came tearing out of those sacks barking and yappin' at me.

Only, he never did.

After a long time, my curiosity got the best of me. I couldn't figure why he was being so quiet.

So, real careful, I leaned over the edge of the grain

bin. With the handle of the pitchfork, I lifted some of the sacks.

What I saw was enough to make me sick.

The pup was there, all right. Nestled down in a place he'd hollowed out under the sacks. Only, he didn't look much like the pup that had chased me up on the haystack just two days ago.

He was real skinny. His little head was laid over in the hay. And it seemed all he could do to raise it and look up at me. Those bright, mischievous eyes of his didn't dance and sparkle when he looked up. They looked sad. Empty. Almost hollow, like he'd given up hope.

It was easy to tell from the first look what was wrong with him.

The little pup was might-near starved to death.

He was so thin, I could count his ribs. And after he looked up at me, he had to put his head back down. That's how weak he was.

Like I said, the sight of him almost made me sick. I don't like dogs, but he didn't look much like a dog, anymore. He looked like something almost dead. An animal hurting. Suffering. And I couldn't help feeling sorry for him, even if he was a dog.

I hated to see an animal suffer. But maybe it was for the best. He darn sure couldn't stay around here. And if we ran him off, he'd only starve to death someplace else. Maybe it was better for him to just die, now.

I grabbed the bucket of oats and headed out of the barn. He whimpered at me as I walked off, as if he was begging me to come back. To help him.

I didn't look back.

I knew what I was doing was for the best.

Chapter 6

It's funny how you make your mind up to a certain thing, then turn right around and change it.

For some reason, I couldn't sleep that night. Every time I closed my eyes, I could see that skinny little pup, looking at me with his big, sad, brown eyes. And when I pulled the pillow around my head and tried to sleep, I could hear that weak, whimpering whine of his, begging for help.

So, a little past midnight, I snuck out of bed and went downstairs. It was dark in the kitchen. But with the yard light on outside, I could see my way to the icebox. There I got a big bowl of milk and bacon, cheese, and bologna scraps left over from the day's meals. Then I stumbled around on the back porch until I found the flashlight Dad kept on the cabinet next to the deep freeze.

The walk up to the barn was kinda spooky, late at night. I could imagine all sorts of things lurking outside the shadowed light of the yard lamp. Coyotes and bobcats. Even a mountain lion. But I wasn't scared with the flashlight in my hand. If I heard any sounds, all I had to do was shine the light to see what it was.

The pup was in the grain bin, where I'd last seen him. He whimpered a bit when I walked up and shined the light on him.

I stood there a while, just to make sure he wasn't gonna jump up and bark at me. Then, I knelt down and scooted the bowl of milk up close to his head.

"Listen, dog," I said. "I still don't have any use for you. I hate dogs, understand. It's only . . . well . . . I don't even want to watch a *dog* starve to death."

He whined and tried to raise his head. All he could do was kinda cock one ear. I scooted the bowl up so close that it bumped him. But he was still so weak he couldn't raise up to get at it.

"I don't like doing this," I said and felt the shivers run down my arm. "But I guess it's the only way to get you to eat."

My arm was shaking somethin' terrible. I managed

to slide a hand under his head. And just knowing he was gonna reach around and bite me, I was ready to take out running if he made the slightest move.

His head felt wobbly in my hand. I raised it up and turned him so his mouth touched the milk.

The minute I turned him, that long, floppy tongue of his snapped out of his mouth, and he went to work. I couldn't help smiling, the way he sucked up the milk faster than you could sneeze. Then, I shoved the meat scraps over. The pup didn't exactly eat the meat—it was more like he was breathing it in. He'd chomp down a double mouthful of bacon and swallow it without even chewing.

It took about ten seconds for him to polish off all the food I brought, and he was still hungry.

All in all, I made four trips to the house for food. That pup ate and ate. Gobbled up that food till I just knew his little, round tummy was gonna pop open at the seams.

He was still whining for more when I left. But I was afraid to give him any more for fear he might blow up.

As I was fixin' to leave, I reached to get the bowl. My hand grazed his nose and that long, pink tongue came floppin' out. All wet and stinky, he licked at the back of my hand. Whined, as if to say "thanks."

I glared down at him. Tried to sound mean.

"Listen, you mangy dog. You don't have anything to thank me for. Soon as you got enough food to get your strength back, I'm running you off. Understand? I don't like you, and I don't want you around. Soon as you're well, that's it! Got me?"

His little tail gave a weak wag. I scowled at him. "I mean it!"

I did, too. Only I guess he didn't believe me.

Way I had things figured, as scraggly and sickly as he looked, it'd probably take two to three days for him to get on his feet again. Then, I'd get a stick or some chunkin' rocks and run his tail clean off our place.

Like I said, my mind was made up. There wasn't anything that could change it.

Three days later, the pup was up on his feet. He looked awful wobbly, though. And I figured if I ran him off, he couldn't get very far.

So I kept feeding him three times a day. Swiping scraps from our table and sticking them in a plastic baggie I stuffed in my pocket. Mama and Dad and Chuckie never did catch me—I was real careful about that. Mama did remark once about how I was eating better.

I just smiled and told her how good the homemade

rolls were. Then, when she turned her head, I stuffed another one into the plastic bag.

The pup enjoyed everything I brought him. Never once did he stick up his nose at any of the scraps. He even liked green beans and corn on the cob.

I can still remember the next time I touched him. It really wasn't my idea. Sometimes, when I'd bring him his food, he'd get to wiggling. Wagging his tail so hard that it shook him clear up to his ears.

I was feeding him scraps of bacon one morning, when he got to wiggling so much he clean knocked himself over. He landed up against my knee, with his fuzzy head against my hand.

Course, I was on my feet and gone in a second. Clean up on top of the grain bin, fast as I could scoot.

Only, the shaking and being afraid didn't take hold of me like I figured. I wasn't trembling all over. I wasn't going through that sick feeling in my stomach that I usually got whenever I was around a dog.

This time, it was different.

"You stay back," I warned as I climbed down from the grain bin. "Eat and leave me alone or I'll, I'll . . ."

I couldn't figure anything mean enough to finish the threat with. Besides, he'd already gone back to the bacon.

It was two days later that I finally got up the courage to touch him on purpose.

It took a lot of doing. My hand was shaking somethin' terrible when I touched his fuzzy back. I yanked it away real quick, only, this time, I didn't run. I didn't climb up to the safety of the grain bin, either.

Instead, I touched him again.

For about a week, I felt big and brave as anything. I figured, just by touching him, I was all over the fear and panic that had hung onto me for so long.

The real test was yet to come.

Mama's meat loaf was about the most favorite thing that pup could sink his teeth into. Even before I'd dump it out of the plastic sack into his feed bowl, he knew it was coming. He'd start bouncing around and yapping.

This one time, I got tickled at the way he was acting and got to giggling. That only made him wiggle and yap more.

I sat down beside the bowl and started to dump the meat loaf. All of a sudden, he bounced around a couple of times and landed square in my lap. I froze, stiff as a rock, didn't even breathe.

He got real still, too. Nothing moved except his eyes (which were on the meat loaf) and his tail (which couldn't stop wagging even if he wanted it to).

Finally, I got up enough courage to give him a good push. He went sliding on his nose across the feed sacks and into the bowl. And, before I could so much as blink, he came runnin' back and plopped in my lap again.

I started to give him another shove. But, for some reason, I reached into the plastic sack and got out a piece of meat loaf.

Be my luck for him to chew my hand off when I offered the meat to him. I closed my eyes. He took it from me so light, I didn't even feel his long, floppy tongue.

The next day, I fed him by hand again. And the next, and the next.

During those days, I never once told myself that I was gonna keep him. I never said, "I got me a dog, now, and he'll help me so I won't be scared anymore."

I never said or thought any of that stuff.

Each day, as I walked up the hill to the barn, I'd tell myself that he was probably strong enough that I could run him off. I'd get the pitchfork or a leather strap or some rocks. And I'd run him off, once and for all.

Then, I'd get to the barn, and he'd be all wiggly

and excited over what I'd brought him. He'd lick my hand and try to crawl up in my lap, and I'd end up shoving and playing with him, giggling and laughing all the while. Then I'd leave the barn and tell myself that *tomorrow* I'd run him off.

Only tomorrow was the same thing. And so was the tomorrow after that.

I never planned to keep him—that's for sure! It was just one of those things that happened. I still don't recollect how.

Chapter 7

I don't rightly remember the pup changing into a dog. I do remember that just about the time school ended, he came up to about my knees. He was still kinda scraggly looking. And he still spent most of his time wagging that fuzzy tail. So, I kept telling myself he was only a pup. Only, inside, I guess I knew better.

Reckon Mama and Dad knew about the pup all along.

Dad didn't come to the barn much 'cause it was summer and there was no need to fetch hay to the cows. But, a couple of times when Beauty and the pup and I would go riding, we'd see him in the truck or on the tractor. We kept our distance, but Dad would have had to be blind not to see him.

He never mentioned dogs or being afraid after that night we had the big fight. Not one word was said, and he did seem easier to get along with.

Mama always fixed a little extra food, especially meat loaf. She managed to leave the table long enough for me to tuck some scraps away in my pocket, yet never seemed to notice when food was missing. And every day, she waited till I was inside the barn before she'd call the cats to come eat.

Somehow, that dumb ole pup got the notion that whenever Mama called "Here, kitty, kitty, kitty" that meant it was suppertime.

It didn't matter, though, 'cause each time she clanged the cat pans together and called them, I was feeding the pup.

Then, one day, it happened.

I was either early feeding him, or Mama was late feeding the cats.

Either way, when she clanged the pans together and called "Here kitty, kitty," his saggy ears perked up and his tail went to waggin'.

Before I could yell, he lit out for the door. I made a flyin' tackle for him. All I got for my trouble was a mouthful of dusty hay and the air knocked out of me.

I came up spitting and coughing and gagging for air. Then, I scrambled to my feet, still hoping I could catch the pup before Mama saw him.

It was easy to tell what was happening long before I got to the house. There was squealing and spittin' and yapping, more noise than you ever heard. The commotion was coming from beside the back door and, right off, I could tell that pesky pup was mixin' with the cats.

Mama was yellin'. And just as I got to the gate, Dad came running out to help her. He had the broom in his hand, raised high for hittin'. But when he saw what was happening, he put the broom down. Leaned back against the wall and went to laughing.

When I saw what was happening, I couldn't help laughing, either.

As the pup started after the food, the cats must have remembered him. They figured he was still too little and cowardly to give them any trouble so, when he came running up, they went after him. The pup had changed considerable from the way he had been.

I was just opening the gate when the first of our six cats whizzed under my legs. She was all fuzzed up, scared, and running like the devil himself had a hold on her tail.

The other five were still wrapped up with the pup. There was hair flying and squalling till I could hardly hear myself think. Mostly, the cats were the ones makin' the noise.

Little wonder, either.

All of a sudden, I saw the pup chomp down on one of the cats. He grabbed her by the back and pitched her straight up in the air. That crazy cat must have flown a good six feet, straight up. She was spinning and squealing. Legs and tail doing kind of a flip-flop, trying to get her balance. She lit with a thud that looked for a second like it broke her in pieces.

Then, the next second she was on her feet running like mad for a nearby locust tree.

Another of the cats was giving the fight to the pup. She came whizzing past so close, it nearly knocked me down. Right behind her came another running scared with its tail puffed up as big around as it was long.

Just the calico and the tomcat were left. The pup shook the tom real hard, and he threw the fight. Took out running like the others.

Only, he was right scared and mixed up after being shook. He must have lost his bearings for a minute. He aimed straight for the house. Mama saw him coming, but she was too slow to do anything about it.

The cat was so confused, he must have thought Mama was a tree. And a tree was the natural place for him when a dog was chasing him.

First thing you know, he shot under Mama's dress and started climbing. Mama went to screaming and jumping up and down like frog legs fryin' in a pan. She kept up her squealing and jumping long after the cat had left her and taken out through the wheat field.

It must have scared the cat more than it did Mama. What with the dog and Mama both ganging up on him like they did, we never did see that cat again.

The calico was hanging fast to the pup's head. She was all balled up on his back. Diggin' in with her claws and chomping a mouthful of ear.

The pup was about ready to give up. He was shaking his head and running in a wide circle that brought him almost to the fence, then back again toward the house. Before I could even think about helping him out, the pup took care of things himself.

Right about to the back door, he stopped. Ducked his head real low, then reared up on his back feet like a bucking bronco and gave a mighty shake of his head. Sure enough, it threw the cat loose. And as the cat was falling, the pup grabbed her by the tail. Shook it a good one, then flung her across the yard.

As if that wasn't enough for the poor cat, she had to go and land on the cellar door. It was a heavy door made out of wood and covered on the outside with sheet metal.

Like most cats, this one lit on her feet. But she was still fighting mad and had her claws out. When those claws hit that slick sheet metal, there wasn't anything for her to do but slide.

She started sliding backwards. And when she started sliding, she started running, trying to get away from the pup.

Only, the more she ran, the more she slid.

She ran and slid and fell and ran some more and slid some more, till I figured she was plumb gonna run herself to death before she got off that slick door.

Finally, she fell and slid off the door. When her feet hit solid ground, she tore out for the barn. Ran so hard, she didn't even notice when she left a big chunk of hair on the fence where she tried to squeeze under.

The pup chased her. But for only a little way.

Then, he came back. Took one bite of the food. And changed completely.

He'd been all business. The hair on his back was bristled up, ready for fight. His lips were bared back, showing white teeth, and there was a vicious glare in his eye.

After one bite of the cat's food, his hair went down across the ridge of his back. His tail started wagging and his long, pink tongue came rolling out of his mouth.

After a second or so, he spotted me over by the gate. Then here he came. He was kinda grinnin' out of one side of his face. Squirmin' and wigglin' till I thought he was gonna fall down.

He stopped at my feet. Barked a couple of times, like he expected me to praise and make over him for the great battle he'd just won.

I did.

After I'd petted him and loved him up good, he trotted back to the food. Not to eat, just to stand guard over it and make sure those pesky cats didn't come back.

It was about then when I noticed Mama and Dad.

Dad had been leaning up against the wall, chuckling. When I saw him now, he was sitting against that wall, right where he'd slid down. He was holding his stomach and laughing so hard that tears came to his eyes. He'd point to the cellar door, where that cat had done so much sliding. Then he'd point back at Mama, who was still dancing around, looking about despairingly to make sure there weren't anymore cats to come clawin' up her leg.

Mama got downright upset when she saw Dad sitting there laughing at her. She walked over and kicked him on the foot. Shook her finger in his face and jumped all over him about not helping her.

Dad tried to keep a straight face while Mama was blessin' him out, but he just couldn't. Mama'd shake her finger at him. Dad would look real serious. Frown and nod his head like he was really listening. Then his cheeks would puff out and his lips would get to quivering till he couldn't hold it in any longer. He'd bust with a big puff of air and go to laughing again.

Mama finally got disgusted with him and stormed off for the house.

Dad straightened up then. He came over to where I was standing by the gate. The laughing and chuckling left him when he put his hands on my shoulders.

He looked at me, then at the pup, then back at me again.

His mouth opened, but the words never came out.

They didn't need to. I knew what he was saying from his eyes, from the way he stood so tall and straight.

My dad was proud of me.

Chapter 8

We named him Kitty.

I don't reckon it was a name anybody planned sticking him with. It just happened that every time Mama called the cats, that pup come a-runnin'. So, it seemed only natural that if "Kitty" was the name he liked, that's what we called him.

Mama fretted a bit over him being around for the first two weeks. Every time she went outside with the feed bowl, she knew there was gonna be another big fight.

She made it a point to wear pants, or slip a pair of Dad's overalls on over her shorts to make sure one of those cats didn't mistake her leg for a tree again.

Kitty was always real considerate about lettin' the cats get there first. Sometimes, I could see him waiting at the side of the barn until our five cats got to the feed bowl.

Then, here he'd come!

He was at the age where he was growing faster than anything else. His legs were long and, he sometimes got to going so fast, he'd trip over his big feet and go tumbling.

It didn't slow him much. But it did give the cats warning he was after them. They'd take one more mouthful of food and light out for the trees.

I found out that Dad had known about Kitty for some five to six weeks, now. He told me he saw him near the grain bin one day and could tell by his round, fat tummy that somebody'd been feeding him. He also told me that, one day when Beauty and I were out for a ride, he took the pup into town and had the vet give him the shots he needed.

He told me something else at dinner one night that gave me considerable worry and kept me from sleeping good a couple of nights.

"A bunch of the farmers over by Lake Burtschi have gone together and hired a professional trapper. They're putting out things called coyote-getters to rid them of the coyotes and the wild dogs that have been killing some of their stock."

"What's that?" I asked.

Dad frowned.

"What's what?"

"A coyote-getter."

"Oh," he nodded. "Well, it's a tube sort of thing. 'Bout as big around as a shotgun shell, only longer. They bury it in the ground and stake a piece of raw meat to one end."

"Then what?" I interrupted.

"A coyote or a dog comes along and grabs the meat, fixing to eat it. When he does, the stake that the meat's on sets off an explosive charge at the bottom of the contraption. It blows the poison powder called cyanide up into the critter's face. Gets in his mouth and nose and kills him, right quick."

"That sounds like a neat trap," I said. "Bet they get rid of a lot of coyotes that way."

Dad nodded. Then, I couldn't help noticing the strange look on his face when he stared at me.

"It's a good way of gettin' rid of coyotes—or dogs."

I tilted my head with a frown. It took me a minute or two to figure out what he meant.

"You mean, like Kitty?"

He looked real solemn when he nodded his head.

"That's right, son. That pup of yours is always lookin' for a free meal. You and him and your horse have been ranging pretty far from home. Won't be long before you start running in to them coyote-getters.

"I'm tellin' you about them for two reasons. First off, I don't want you fooling around with them. You stumble over one or go to tugging around, trying to see what they look like, you just as liable as a coyote to get a faceful of poison. You can usually spot where they are 'cause the trappers put out a stake with a red ribbon on them someplace near the trap. You see a piece of ribbon like that, you steer clear, understand?"

"Yes, sir." I could tell by his voice that Dad wasn't foolin'.

He kinda cleared his throat and went on. "Only trouble is, I can't explain the stuff about the ribbon to Kitty. That pup of yours finds himself a piece of free meat, he wouldn't bother to look and see if there was a flag around. He'd just grab it and end up gettin' himself killed."

I sank down in my chair. Bit at my lip.

"We could stay closer to the house," I said. "Just ride on our place and steer clear of the neighbors."

Dad nodded.

"Yeah. But that won't keep the pup from wandering. A fence don't mean nothing to a dog. Once school starts, he's gonna wander out on his own trying to find something to do until you come home."

Dad kinda sat back in his chair. Frowned and

scratched at his chin like he was thinking hard on something.

"Might not hurt if we fixed up a pen to put him in when school starts."

I was up on the edge of my chair.

"I bet it'd work, Dad. I'll help you build it."

It sounded like a good idea. We told Mama 'bout it, and she agreed. Everybody thought it was right smart.

Everybody except Kitty.

Dad and I had the pen finished by the first day of school. It was about six thirty when I had to get up. The school bus came from Chickasha about seven thirty, and I wanted to give myself plenty of time to get Kitty in the pen and make sure he was all right before I left.

Kitty was easy enough to catch. He always came when I called him. But when I opened the gate to put him in the pen, it was a different story.

The cage was made out of hog wire. We put it up with fence posts and sloshed cement around the bottom so Kitty couldn't dig out. It was about six feet square and had a barrel with a hole cut in one end near the back of the pen. I'd stuffed the barrel with fresh, clean hay so Kitty could make himself a bed.

When he finally figured I was trying to stuff him

into that pen, he threw a regular wall-eyed fit. He started squalling and twisting around, like I was trying to kill him. He yowled and jumped, trying to get away.

I latched onto his ear and hung on for dear life. For a minute, I figured he was gonna yank away and I'd be standing there, holding his ear. Only Kitty's ears were a mite sensitive so, after a bit more jumping and trying to yank away, he went to whimpering and settled down.

I shoved him inside the pen with my foot and latched the gate.

The look he gave was one of those things I'll never forget. It was like I was his best friend and, all of a sudden, I'd double-crossed him. Stabbed him in the back, or kicked him in the teeth, just when he was trusting me with all his heart.

He whimpered and whined, begging me to let him out. I knew I couldn't, though, so I walked off. His yowling and whining followed me to the house. And after I got my stuff for school, I could still hear him begging me to let him out, all the way to where I met the bus.

Generally, the first day of school is a pretty exciting thing. New friends to make. Old buddies from last year to talk to and play with at recess. New teachers to try and figure out, see what kind of stuff they'll let you get away with.

Fifth grade was even more exciting than last year. In Chickasha, all the fifth and sixth graders go to Intermediate School. And instead of just one teacher, we had six. Just about the time I'd get settled in a room, get good and relaxed, the bell would ring, and I'd have to grab all my books and go hunting my next class.

Brad and I didn't have any classes together in the morning. I did see him in the hall once. We only had a second or two to talk. It was long enough to find out that we had lunch period at the same time. We agreed that whoever got in the lunchroom first would save the other a seat.

I was might near busting at the seams to tell Brad about my new dog.

"You're kiddin'!" He almost choked on the buttered roll.

I smiled. Held my shoulders back, real proud of myself.

"No. I really do. His name's Kitty."

Brad's eyes scrunched up tight, studying me. He had the good manners to finish swallowing his roll before he started in again.

"You're kiddin'," he repeated.

I shook my head.

"No. Honest."

"Where'd he come from? Your dad buy him for you? How long you had him? Why'd you name him Kitty? What kind is he? How big . . ."

By the time I got all his questions answered and convinced him I honestly had a dog, the recess bell rang, and it was time for us to head to class again.

Just outside the door, Brad stopped. There was a special kinda look in his eyes. A smile that made me feel sorta warm inside.

"I knew you weren't a coward," he said. "I knew, once you set your mind to it, you'd get over being scared."

He drew back and slugged me on the shoulder.

"Save me a place at lunch tomorrow," he called as he disappeared into the crowd pushing through the door.

The warm, proud feeling I had lasted clear through the next class. But, during social studies, I got to thinking about Kitty and that hurt look on his face when I left this morning. Kept hearing his whining, begging me to let him come along.

Chances were, he wouldn't be very happy to see me when I got home. He might not want anything to do with me after the way I treated him this morning.

After a while, I made myself downright miserable worrying about him not liking me anymore.

When the bus stopped on the road in front of my house, I found out there'd been no need to worry about my pup.

He was waiting for me by the windmill. His tail was wagging clean up to his long floppy tongue. He came bouncing to greet me. Jumped up so hard it almost knocked the wind out of me.

"How'd you get out?" I demanded.

Kitty only slopped me across the hand with his wet tongue. I rubbed his ears and pushed him back.

"I'm glad you didn't get into any of that poison Dad was talking about. How'd you get out?"

He jumped up on me again. I laughed. He made it a regular game, jumping up and me pushing him back so he could jump on me again.

I was glad to know that he'd forgiven me for puttin' him in the pen. But I was sure curious how he got out.

When we got back to Kitty's pen, Dad was there. He was standing on a ladder, putting some new fence on the top of the cage.

"You named that pup of yours good and proper," he chuckled when we walked up. "He doesn't only come when you call 'Here Kitty, kitty.' He climbs better than most of the cats we got. I put him back in this pen three times after you left, and each time he climbed right out."

"You mean over the top?" I wondered, looking at how high the fence was.

Dad nodded.

"That's right. Think this'll hold him, though."

Dad tied the last strand of wire in place. Now the cage had a top on it. I knew there wasn't any way for Kitty to get out come tomorrow.

Only tomorrow, he dug out under the cement we poured around the bottom of the pen. The day after that, he kept jumping on the gate till he jarred the latch loose. And Friday, he gnawed through the leather strap Dad had him tied up with.

"It's no use," Dad told me early Saturday morning. "We've tried everything I can think of to keep that pup of yours in. Guess we'll just have to give up. Hope he doesn't get into any of the poison the farmers got spread around."

I couldn't argue with Dad about that. There just wasn't any way to keep Kitty penned up. With all the red flags I saw when Beauty and I went riding Saturday afternoon, that began to worry me plenty.

Dad had said the red ribbons marked the places where the coyote-getters were planted. Some of them were right up against the fence to our place.

Once, after we'd been riding for about two hours and were headed home, I caught Kitty sniffing around where one of them was set. Beauty and I had to practically run over him to get him away from it.

I still told myself I hated dogs. Only, I never really counted Kitty as a dog. I had come to think quite a bit of my scraggly pup. And I just knew if I didn't come up with something soon, it was only a matter of time before he got to snooping around one of those traps and got himself killed.

I didn't love him, but I didn't want my pup to get killed, either.

Chapter 9

It was a week later, at suppertime, when I finally came up with a plan for keeping Kitty away from the poison meat.

Chuckie was sitting in his chair across from me. He was five, now. And he'd been trying to act real grown up since he started kindergarten this year. He didn't squeal and whine like when he was little. His table manners were better, too. He didn't slop around in his food anymore, and it'd been weeks since he'd turned his drink over and splashed it across the table.

I wasn't paying him much attention this evening, 'cause I was still figurin' on a way to protect my pup.

Then, all of a sudden, Chuckie set up a howl like I hadn't heard since he was three. He went to screaming and crying like he was about to die.

Before anybody knew what was happening, he turned his plate over. Spilled milk in the mashed potatoes and liked to yanked the tablecloth off the table when he jumped up.

He went screaming through the house. Mama took a big scare, seeing him act like that. So, she took out after him, trying to catch him to see what was wrong.

It scared me some, too. Even if he was my little brother, always getting into my stuff and messin' up my room, even if he never minded me when I told him to do something, like I said, he was still my brother. And I could tell by the way he was crying that he was hurt. From the fuss he was settin' up, I was afraid he was hurt bad, even though I didn't know what hurt him.

Dad was worried, too. We got up and started off after Mama and Chuckie. Mama chased him around the house, twice, before she finally caught up with him.

He was hurt and squealing mad. Kicking and crying and trying to hold onto Mama for comfort. Dad and I gathered around them.

It took Mama a long time to pet and love him till he calmed down.

"What is it, Chuckie?" she kept asking. "Where's my little boy hurt? What's wrong?"

Finally, Chuckie calmed down enough that he caught his breath. With a shaking hand, he pointed at his mouth.

"It's hot," he cried. "Somethin' real hot."

Mama frowned at Dad. And Dad frowned at me. I shrugged, not knowing what Chuckie meant, either.

"Hot!" Chuckie whined again.

Dad slapped himself on the leg.

"Why that little thief," he said. "I bet he . . ."

Dad never finished his sentence. He turned and trotted off for the kitchen. I figured he was on to something, so I followed. Mama, still fussin' and making over Chuckie, picked him up and followed us, too.

Dad was in the kitchen when we found him. Mama and I kept looking at each other, real puzzled like. Dad was diggin' through the gooey mess of mashed potatoes and milk in Chuckie's plate. All at once, he let out a sly chuckle. Slapped his leg.

"Just what I figured. Look here."

Mama and I frowned. He held up a bright, green colored little thing. Shook it back and forth.

"That little scamp must have reached over in my plate and swiped this while I wasn't watchin'."

Mama tilted her head.

"What is it?"

Dad laughed.

"Hot pepper."

"Hot pepper," she squawked. "Well, no wonder . . ."

Chuckie was still whimpering. When he saw the green pepper Dad was holding up, his eyes got real big and he started crying again.

"Hot!" he complained.

I felt my face kinda wrinkle up with sympathy for the little fella. I'd latched onto one of Dad's hot peppers before, back when I was younger and didn't know better. I could still remember the burning, like I'd swallowed a mouthful of fire. That thing burned clean from my lips to the bottom of my stomach.

Dad took Chuckie from Mama. He held him under the arms and kinda pitched him in the air a couple of times.

"Come on, son. I know what'll take care of that old pepper."

He got Chuckie a piece of bread and a glass of milk. When he'd gobbled that down, Dad got the ice cream out of the freezer, and we all had a bowl.

When we'd finished, Mama started scraping the scraps off our plates into the bowls to feed Kitty and the cats.

"Be sure you get the rest of that pepper out of

Chuckie's plate," Dad warned. "Those cats will go climbing up every tree in the country if they catch hold of that pepper."

That's when the idea hit me.

I felt my eyes kinda pop wide open. Then a smile tugged at the corners of my mouth.

"Hey, Dad. Can I have a couple of your peppers?"

Dad frowned. Leaned his head way to the side.

"You musta forgot the last time you tried one of those, Ricky. You acted might near like Chuckie. Danced around the house for ten minutes, yowling and complaining how hot your mouth was."

"I remember, Dad. Only it's not for me."

He tilted his head the other way.

"What do you want 'em for?"

I smiled.

"Kitty."

Mama turned away from the sink where she was doing the dishes.

"That pup's got more sense than to eat one of those things."

"Not if I wrap it up in some hamburger meat," I answered. "The way he gobbles his food, he wouldn't even stop to sniff it."

Dad shook his head.

"That's mighty cruel to pull on that pup," he said sternly.

"We've always tried to teach you to be kind to

animals," Mama jumped in. "A trick like that isn't right. It's . . ."

I waved my hand, trying to cut them off.

"It is a mighty cruel thing to do," I agreed. "Only it's not a trick. It's serious business."

Dad folded his arms across his stomach.

"Just what do you mean, 'Serious business?' "

I leaned across the table. Twisted Dad's jar of hot peppers in my hands.

"You know how you were telling me about those trappers baiting them coyote-getters with raw meat?"

"Yeah."

"Well, I was just thinking. We can't keep Kitty in a pen or tied up. It's just a matter of time before he finds him some of that meat and gets in the traps, right?"

Dad nodded.

"I'm afraid so."

I felt my smile gettin' bigger.

"We can't keep him from roaming around, but what if we could keep him from messin' with the meat he finds around those traps?"

Dad's frown suddenly changed to a grin when he figured out what I was talking about.

"You mean, set out some meat for him and load it with hot peppers?"

I nodded.

"Yes. Then, when he eats it, he'll get a dose of what Chuckie got. Maybe, that way, he won't be eating meat and stuff unless it's in his bowl."

Dad took the jar of hot peppers and laid two of them on a plate.

"Sounds like it just might work. Worth a try, anyhow."

I told Mama to wait a while to call the cats to eat. I took the first wad of hamburger and laid it near the path Kitty always took when he came running from the barn for his food. The second one, I laid out by Beauty's pen. I knew Kitty'd find it there when Beauty and I went riding later this evening.

Dad figured Kitty might get wise to the hamburger, so he had Mama cut up some raw steak and we loaded it with peppers, too.

Kitty did just like we figured.

Mama banged the pans together and yelled, "Here, kitty, kitty, kitty."

I could see him waiting by the edge of the barn. He stood there, just like always, waiting for the cats to come to the house first. Mama had been feeding them on top of the screened-in back porch. But I figure Kitty was still planning for them to get into his feed bowl, and he wanted to give them the chance to get there first so he could run 'em off.

The cats knew his tricks, though. So, when he saw them climbing up on the screen to get on top of the porch where their own bowl was, he came on to the house.

The ball of hamburger meat was sittin' beside the path that led from the barn to the back gate.

At first, I thought Kitty was gonna ignore the meat. Then, after he'd passed it, he came to a screeching stop. Sniffed the air a couple of times and turned back.

Sure enough, he found the hamburger. He grabbed it. Kinda pitched it in the air and opened his mouth real big. Gulped it down without hardly chewin'. Then, to my surprise, he came trottin' on to the house like nothin' whatsoever was wrong.

With a frown, I scratched at my head.

"You reckon the pepper fell out 'fore he got it?"

Dad only smiled.

"Just give it time. That thing just hasn't hit bottom, yet."

Kitty squeezed under the gate. He took a look around to make sure there weren't any cats within reach, then he trotted on to his feed bowl.

All at once, he stopped dead in his tracks.

His floppy ears perked up, almost straight over his head. Then, he doubled over. Looked between his front legs, like to see if there were ants or somethin' chewin' on his belly.

That hot pepper must have really hit him, then.

He started shaking his head. Diggin' at his mouth with both paws like he'd got him a mouthful of bumblebees. He went to howlin' and yelpin'. Jumping up in the air and turning a complete circle before he hit the ground.

I felt sorry for him. But even feelin' sorry for him, I had to slap my hand over my mouth to keep from laughing at the way he was acting.

He'd flop over on his back with his feet kickin' in the air. Then he'd jump up and start turning circles. All of a sudden he'd fall over and start pawin' at his mouth again. Yowlin' and howlin' all the time.

Dad was doubled over laughing. Mama kinda got onto both of us, sayin' how mean we were to that poor old pup. But all the time she was scolding us, I could see that kinda twinkle in her eye and the way she had to fight the corners of her mouth to keep from smiling.

It wasn't long 'fore Mama took pity on him. She went inside and came back with a big bucket full of water.

Kitty was still pitchin' and reelin' around. But when he saw the water bucket, he came on the run.

In all my days, I never saw an animal drink so

much water. He must have stood there with his long, floppy tongue in that bucket for thirty minutes. He'd stop now and then to catch his breath, then he'd go right back to drinking.

When he was through, I could swear I heard his stomach slosh as he walked.

It took him three days before he got into the meat again. This time, it was one of the pieces of steak I'd hid around the house.

About bedtime one evening, we heard his yowling and howling outside. Dad went to look and when he came back, he asked if I'd hid any of the meat by the air conditioner.

I told him I had, and he said that Kitty had found it.

After that, we never had anymore trouble with Kitty snitchin' strange meat. The three other pieces of meat I had stashed around the place were left untouched. I don't even reckon he sniffed them. He'd eat hamburger in his feed bowl, but he always smelled it real good first.

The big test came around Thanksgiving vacation.

Beauty and Kitty and I hadn't done much riding 'cause school kept me pretty busy. I'd ride some in the afternoons, but we never managed to get very far from the house.

In November, we had a four-day vacation for Thanksgiving. The first morning out of school, Beauty and I took off to see some of the country.

Kitty came along, too. Lately, he'd found that there were birds running around. Quail is what Dad called them. He said they were a game bird and that Kitty looked to him like he was part Irish Setter, a good hunting breed.

Anyhow, Kitty would go sniffin' through the tall brown blades of fall grass and sooner or later stumble on a bunch of these quail.

I watched him once. He came along all crouched down. Then, when he was right on them, he'd jump up and land in the middle of the bunch.

'Course, he never caught anything. They always flew just the second before he landed. Beating their wings and drumming the crisp fall air as they scattered every which way.

Kitty liked to chase after them. But when he figured he'd ranged far enough, he'd circle back to Beauty and me.

It was during one of these sniffin' hunts for birds that he stumbled across the coyote-getter.

Just like Dad said, there was a stick with a red ribbon nearby. All you could see of the trap, though, was a big chunk of raw meat, free for the taking.

When I saw what Kitty was sniffin' at, I yanked

Beauty around and headed back. My heart sank clean down to the bottom of my stomach, 'cause I realized Beauty and I were too far away. There was no way I could save my pup if he took a notion to eat some free beef. We couldn't reach him in time. One bite and he'd be dead before we got there.

Kitty had learned his lesson from the hot peppers. I held my breath as he sniffed the meat. Then laughed out loud when he heisted his leg and peed on it.

Kitty had a way of expressin' himself, tellin' everybody just what he thought about that meat.

I never worried about him gettin' into the traps after that day. And after Thanksgiving vacation, I didn't feel a bit bad about going back to school. It didn't worry me to leave him, 'cause I knew he'd be all right while I was gone.

Chapter 10

By the week before Christmas break, I was so all-fired excited I couldn't sit still in my desk. All I could think about was riding Beauty and playing and eating the good holiday food Mama'd fix.

By the time Christmas vacation came, I was ready for some adventures and excitement. Things had been pretty boring around our farm. I hadn't had much time to ride Beauty and roam with my pup. I'd been too busy helpin' Dad with the cattle.

I was about to pop when the bus dropped me off after the last day of school.

Kitty was waiting for me by the windmill, like usual. I was pretty good about dodging out of the way before he jumped on me. But today I let him jump up and put his paws on my chest and lick my face. Then we headed off for the house at a run. All the way I kept tellin' Kitty about the fun things we were gonna do now that I was out of school for a couple of weeks.

When I reached the house and went running in to put up my books and the Christmas things I'd made at school, all my excitement and feeling good and being happy just whooshed out of me.

Dad was on the telephone. Mama shushed me the second I came in the door. I could tell by the look on their faces that something was wrong. Something serious.

I kinda held my breath, trying to be real quiet.

Dad was ending up his talking on the phone. He nodded his head. Frowned.

"Let me call you back, Martha. I'll see what I can do."

Then he hung up the phone and kinda sank down in the chair. Mama went over and put a hand on his shoulder. Smoothed his hair back off his forehead.

"How bad is he?" she said. "Are the kids all right?"

Dad shook his head. I could see a tear roll down his cheek. He tried to wipe it away.

"Martha said Ben was in critical condition. He's got a concussion and multiple fractures. He's in a coma, and the doctors won't tell her what his chances are . . ." Dad cleared his throat. "Alex and Theresa were with him when they had the wreck. Alex is dead. Theresa's just got a broken leg and a scratch on her arm. Guess being in the back seat is what saved her."

I could see Dad's bottom lip quivering. See how hard it was for him to keep from crying.

"Martha said she would have been with them. But she got a touch of the flu and stayed at the house."

He stopped then. Mama sat on his lap and snuggled him up. Kissing him on the cheeks and holding him tight.

Martha was Dad's sister—my aunt. It had been a long time since we had seen them and their two kids, Alex and Theresa. I was only about Chuckie's age when we last went to visit—so I didn't remember them very well at all. But watching how bad Dad was hurting over what had happened, I couldn't help hurting, too.

I went over and sat down on his lap beside Mama. Loved him up like she was doing. Tried to make him feel better.

Finally, Mama said, "Is there anything we can do? Any way we can help her?"

Dad bit down on his lip.

"She asked me to come. She wants me to be with her. Help . . . but . . . I just don't see how," he stammered. "I . . . I don't see how I can get away. There's so much needs done 'round here. We got three heifers comin' in with calves anytime, now. And with the snow that's supposed to come soon, I'll have to haul hay to the ones we got out on pasture, and . . ."

Mama got up on her feet. She patted him on the leg, then, holding his hands, helped him up.

"Nonsense, Nick. Your sister needs you, and you got to go. Ricky and I can take care of the cows. Let's go get your clothes packed."

She took his hand and led him toward the stairs. Dad stopped and pulled his hand from hers.

"That's too much for you to handle alone, Helen," he said. "I just better call Martha and tell her . . ."

"No!" Mama's stern tone cut him short. "She's your only sister. And after losing her only son and maybe her husband in a car wreck, Martha needs you. You'd feel guilty from now on if you didn't go."

"I'll feel guilty about leaving you with all the work to do around here," he argued. "There's too much liftin' and pullin' and straining. If you wear yourself out and get sick, I'd never forgive myself."

Mama stood up on her tiptoes and kissed his cheek.

"Us womenfolk have been liftin' and pullin' and strainin' 'bout as long as menfolk. Besides, I've got Ricky to help me. He's pretty stout for a ten-year-old and what I can't handle, I'm sure he can."

I rushed over beside them.

"That's right, Dad. I been with you to feed the cattle. I know how much to give them, and I can lift hay bales, might near as good as you."

"And I've watched you pull calves before," Mama added. "And I know the signs of milk fever, if I need to call the vet. Now, your sister needs you. Ricky and I can manage for a few days while you're gone."

"But . . ." Dad started in again.

Mama put her fingers to his lips.

"Now, hush. No more argument. Let's get you packed and then we'll call Martha to tell her you're on your way."

Dad knew when he was licked.

He followed Mama upstairs without another word.

When they were gone, my head was all in a spin. There had never been a bad car wreck with anybody I knew before. I guess it's something that happens so fast and unexpected, it just takes time for your head to take it all in. Takes time for your mind to catch up with the way your heart's poundin' and the way all sorts of feelings go floodin' through.

A car wreck is a bad thing. And Dad leaving us, even if it was for just a few days, well . . . that was a bad thing, too.

I sat down on the couch and turned the TV on. It didn't help much, though.

What did help was when Chuckie finished playing in his room and came down, wanting me to help with his school stuff. His kindergarten class was studyin' letters. He wanted me to write some letters on some paper. Then, he'd try to tell me what the letters were and write them by himself on another piece of paper.

He did pretty good with most of them, only he kept getting the little *b, p,* and *d* all mixed up.

Working with him kept both of us busy. Kept our minds off Dad.

Chuckie and I worked on letters while Mama was fixin' supper. And after we finished eating, Mama told Chuckie to put on his big coat, and we set out to do the chores.

Feedin' was a snap. Dad had the truck filled with hay and, the first time out, all we had to do was drive through the pasture and pitch it.

Mama drove the truck, and I sat in the back. I'd use the wire cutters to snap the bailing wire, then pitch it out, chunk at a time. That way, the cows were all spread out and could eat without buttin' one another and fighting over the hay.

Havin' 'em spread out made it easier to count and look 'em over. We checked to make sure there were no bad wire cuts and none of them were sick.

Three cows were ready to have calves. Countin'

was special important with that going on. Dad says it never fails that when their baby's ready to come, they'll wander off from the rest of the bunch. Find a nice private place to bring a fresh new life into this world.

Sure enough, the second day Dad was gone, we came up one heifer short. Mama and I counted twice, just to make sure, then we headed off for the rock hill to see if she was all right.

I found her holed up in a plum thicket near some big, red sandstone boulders. Her new calf was with her, already standing on his wobbly legs and trying to get some milk.

I figured the smart thing to do was herd her back to the small pen by the house. That way, we could keep an eye on her and the baby. Make sure they were all right and not have to prowl around the rock hill trying to find where she and the calf were hidin' next time.

Kitty was with me, so I decided to send him in after her.

"Go get her, boy. Bring 'em out for me."

Kitty cocked his ears and gave me a funny look.

"Go on," I urged. "Go bring 'em out."

I pointed, and he just looked at me real dumb, like. Well, we'd never worked cows together, so I figured he didn't know what I was wanting him to do.

I picked up a stick and started into the plum thicket, pounding the brush as I went.

"Come on, Kitty. All you got to do is go barkin' and chase her out the other side. We're gonna herd her back to the house."

I was so proud I nearly popped. Kitty and I were about halfway into the thicket when he seemed to catch on to the game we were playing. He started barking. Went tearing ahead of me toward the cow. I figured he was gonna run her out and take her clear to the lot. All I'd have to do was follow.

Only, when Kitty came face to face with that old cow, the cow didn't run. Instead, she ducked her head. Threatened by shaking her horns back and forth in his face.

Kitty barked at her some more. Made her snort and paw at the ground.

Then, before I knew what was happening, she charged him.

Kitty yelped and came running back to me for protection. And here came that mad heifer, right behind. She was running hard. Cracking branches and brush as she ran.

"No, Kitty," I yelled. "Take her the other way!"

Only Kitty wasn't listening. Something big and mean was chasing him, and the only thing he could think of was getting back to me where he'd be safe.

I spun around and lit out. Kitty shot past, so close he nearly knocked my feet out from under me. That left me between Kitty and the mad cow who was chasing him.

I was running hard and scared. I didn't notice that she stopped chasing me when we reached the edge of the plum thicket.

There was a barbed-wire fence about fifty feet away. I ran for it, hard as I could. Made a flying dive like a base runner belly-sliding into home plate. Only then did I take time to see where she was.

The old cow was back in the thicket with her calf. Kitty came trottin' up beside me. Wagging his tail and acting like nearly gettin' run down by a mad cow was nothin' more than a big game.

"You stinkin' coward." I glared at him. "You nearly got me killed. You're nothin' but a . . . a . . . coward."

He tried to jump up on me, and I pushed him back with my knee.

"Some cow dog you are. You're supposed to keep her from gettin' me, not get her to chase me. Dummy."

I still had hopes, though. So we tried the same thing again.

Just like before, Kitty rushed in and got that old heifer all stirred up. And when she chased him, he came straight for me.

This time, though, she didn't stop at the edge of the thicket. She ran me clean to the barbed-wire fence.

Mama and Chuckie finally found us. I guess it was because of all the commotion and yellin' I was doing at Kitty.

I told her what Kitty was doing. She told me to hold on to him so he wouldn't get the cow all excited. Then, she and Chuckie picked up some rocks and started chunking at the plum thicket.

Sure enough, the cow led her calf out the other side and, with Mama and Chuckie throwing rocks behind her, it was no time before we reached the house.

I was right disgusted with my dog. Bringing the cow to the house was somethin' I should have been man enough to do myself. Instead, Mama had to do it with the help of a little five-year-old.

It was downright embarrassing.

Chapter 11

The next few days went pretty fast. Dad called a couple of times from St. Louis to see how we were and to tell Mama that Martha's husband was gettin' better.

We drove out and fed the cows every day. It turned cold, and I used Dad's ax to break the ice on the pond so they could drink.

Then, one night, the weatherman on TV said there was snow coming.

"We'll need to get the chains on the truck," Mama told me. "Better get an early start in the morning."

Mama had watched Dad put the chains on before. But neither one of us had ever done it ourselves. It took over an hour the next day for us to do it.

The snow we got just kept right on coming. For three days it snowed off and on, and the weather stayed cold all that time.

Usually when a snow comes in Oklahoma, it only lasts a day or so before melting. This one acted like it might stay the rest of the winter.

After five days, it finally started to warm up. The snow began melting and got the ground real sloppy.

That's when Mama got the pickup stuck.

We were headed to the pasture with a load of hay. Mama was driving in the low ground between the creek and the rock hill when all of a sudden the truck just kinda sank down. The wheels growled and shot mud high in the air when she pushed on the gas. She tried rocking it back and forth, only the tires just went deeper in the gooey, sticky mud.

I got out and started pushing. Mama didn't see me. Right after I got there, she pushed down on the gas real hard.

Before I could move, I was covered with mud from my face clean down to my boots.

When I closed my mouth, I could feel the gritty, grimy grains of dirt crunching between my teeth. I spit and gagged some before I could get them out.

Mama noticed the commotion. She turned the truck off and came back to help me. She used some rags Dad kept in the truck to dig the mud out of my eyes and ears. Then she helped me wipe off my face.

"I'm . . . I'm sorry," I sputtered. "Guess I'm just not big enough to push you out."

Mama sighed.

"It wasn't your fault. That truck's bogged down clear to the hubcaps. We'll have to wait till your dad gets home and pulls it out with the tractor."

Mama walked around the truck a couple of times. She muttered to herself. Then, hauled off and kicked the old truck hard as she could.

I never dreamed Mama knew the words she let out then. Daddy said things like that when he was special mad at one of the cows or when the tractor wouldn't start. But I never figured Mama knew those kinds of words, too. She called that old truck so many names, I couldn't keep up with them.

When she saw me listening, she slapped a hand over her mouth. I couldn't help noticing the way her face turned red. And how embarrassed and sheepish she looked.

"I ever hear you repeating any of those words," she threatened me, "I'll blister your tail so hard you won't sit down for a week. You understand, young man?"

I felt myself snap to attention. I stood real straight. Real still.

"Yes, mam!"

She looked embarrassed again, then got Chuckie out of the truck and started for the house.

"Just throw the hay out here for them," she said, sloshing across the soggy field. "If those cows are so dumb they can't find it, they can just go without."

After she and Chuckie were gone, I hollered and honked the horn a few minutes. Then I broke the bailing wire on the hay and pitched it out around the truck.

The cows took their sweet time about getting there. I counted twice and still came up one short. That probably meant that another one of the heifers was hid up some place having her calf.

I snuck off from the truck, real quiet, hoping my yelling and honking the horn hadn't brought Kitty on the run. By the time I rounded the far side of the rock hill, I was feelin' right proud of myself for gettin' away without that pesky, good-for-nothing pup trailin' along.

Right about then, I heard a rustling sound behind me. I turned just in time to see Kitty come racin' up. He jumped onto me from behind, and it was all I could do to keep from fallin' flat on my face.

"You stinkin' hound," I growled at him. "Why don't you go back and chase cats or somethin'? I don't need you scarin' that old cow."

He just wagged his tail and tried to jump on me again.

I reached down to grab a rock to pelt him. When I did that, he kinda jumped up and laid his front paws over the back of my neck. Then he started sloppin' me in the face with his long, wet tongue.

"All right," I said, pushing him back. "You can go with me. But if you get that old cow to chasin' me, I'll skin your hide."

I was smilin' at him, but I was still mad inside.

It was gettin' cold. The day had been warm enough to melt some of the snow. But evening was comin' on. With the sun on the other side of the hill, that left me in the shade where the icy north wind chilled me clear to the bone.

Kitty and me hunted most every place I could think of for that old heifer. We looked in the three plum patches, the draw along the creek that flowed from the top of the hill, and finally the big canyon right near the edge of our place where the cotton-wood trees were so thick.

Still, there was no sign of the heifer.

"If that don't beat all," I muttered, trying to sound like Dad did sometimes. "That old cow's really found her a good hiding place."

Kitty perked his ears up, listening.

I frowned at him.

"Why don't you go find her, you worthless mutt? It's gettin' on toward dark. Mama's gonna be worried if we don't get back soon."

Dumb old Kitty just tilted his head and wagged his tail.

I started back around the hill, following the way we came. It was so cold I had to keep moving or I knew I'd freeze. My nose and cheeks hurt. Even with gloves on, I kept rubbing my hands together so they wouldn't get numb.

The cold didn't bother Kitty at all. He kept bouncin' around and waggin' his tail. Pokin' his nose in the tall grass, trying to come up with a quail scent or find him a rabbit to chase.

We were almost back to the pickup before I remembered the pond.

The pond was smack in the middle of the hill, a natural dam of rocks and mud about halfway between the top and the creek at the bottom. During the spring it was so full of water the cows only went there to drink. But during the winter and summer when the water was down, there was a flat draw up at the west end of it. A good flat spot with plenty of cover. It was the perfect place for a spooky old cow to hide out and have her calf.

"Come on, Kitty. Got one more place to check."

I started up the little path, moving fast as I picked

my way through the gnarled brush and over-jagged rocks.

The light was growing dim, and a couple of times I tripped over rocks hidden in the shadows. But Kitty was right behind me. The one time I fell, he rushed up and started loppin' me with his wet tongue, figuring I was down there on the ground to play with him.

That cold, wet tongue got me on my feet in a hurry.

The brush grew thicker the higher up the rock hill. Branches tangled together over the path, and tall, dry love grass stood thick and bushy on either side. Most places I had to walk all stooped over. A couple of times, I had to crawl through the thick, tangled vines on my hands and knees.

It was hard traveling. I had been puffin' and pantin' so hard I didn't notice the quiet until I stood up straight at the clearing beside the dam.

There wasn't a breath of wind.

In Oklahoma, the wind blows a lot. But right at sunset, like it was now, the wind lays a bit. The tree limbs stop their rattling and the dry grass quits its swaying and rustling.

It was kind of a spooky quiet. What with the wind blowing and rustlin' things around all day, to have it stop all of a sudden made the chills creep up my back. The low-hanging clouds didn't help either. It was growing dark, and the gray clouds soaked up what little light was left.

Still, the pond was a pretty place. It was mostly dried up now except for a patch of snow and a little water out in the middle. The ground around it was smooth and clear. Here and there, little tufts of winter grass sprung up, giving their bright green touch of color to the brown trees and red rocks that lay scattered around.

It was a wild place. I couldn't help dreamin' about how pretty it would look in the spring. Then everything would be green. The big trees that lined the pond would give it shade and make fine places for the birds to gather and flutter about.

I was lookin' around, kinda dreamin' to myself, when I heard a noise at my feet.

With a frown, I glanced down. Kitty was growling. The hair on his back was standing in a ragged ridge clean to his tail.

He seemed to tremble a moment. Then he growled again and went chargin' off across the dry pond.

What on earth's got into him, I wondered.

Then, without taking much thought, I chased out after him.

I reckon all along I figured he'd found our missin' heifer. And sure enough, he had. She stood against a rock ledge at the far side of the pond. She had a baby calf with her. Brand-spankin' new and still wet. He must have just been born, 'cause he was wobbly, and he could hardly stand.

I'd never seen Kitty growl and get all ruffled up over a cow before. But I figured he was just like me, so tired of looking for that darned old heifer he was downright mad.

When I found out what Kitty was really growlin' about, it was almost too late.

There was a sound beside me as I moved toward the old cow. I paused. Held my breath, listening.

At first I figured the noise was a rabbit or something. Then the noise came again. I could tell it was way too loud to come from a rabbit.

I followed the sound with my ears. Squinted. Strained my eyes against the shadowy depths of the thick brush.

Something moved.

It was no more than a shadow at first. A big, loping shadow that appeared and disappeared among a thousand other darker shadows.

Then, the form took shape.

I froze in my tracks. The breath caught half in and half out of my throat.

And, I swear that my heart clean stopped beatin' for a full second or more.

The form that came from the shadows was a dog. A huge, lumbering hulk of a dog that moved as silent as cat's feet on a down pillow.

Another sound came. A second dog followed the first. He wasn't as big, but he slinked along, moving among the shadows, followed by another larger dog and another. They were headed for the heifer and her new calf.

But Kitty got there first. He stood square in the mouth of the draw, between the cow and the four dogs that drew closer and closer through the darkening shadows.

Usually friendly and tail-waggin', Kitty bared his teeth. A savage, deep-throated growl rumbled through the stillness of the tiny valley.

The heifer was scared. Her nostrils flared out when she snorted and tossed her head from side to side. She wasn't watchin' Kitty, though. Her eyes, round as dishpans, were on the four dogs.

She bellowed once. Tossed her head, threatening. Then she looked to the other side of the draw.

I was trembling scared. So scared I couldn't take my eyes off where I'd last seen the four dogs in the shadows. But when I saw that scared glaze in her eye, I turned to look.

Another dog stood at the edge of the clearing on my left. He stood perfectly still, almost blending with the rocks and brush behind him.

What frightened me were his eyes. White and big. Sharp, piercing eyes that didn't blink.

Eyes that stared right into me.

He was a German shepherd. About the same size as the others, but not afraid to come out into the clearing instead of hiding in the shadows.

He stared straight at me. Watched. Waited.

The others hadn't seen me. They were intent on the newborn calf. But this big shepherd saw me, all right.

His lips curled back, baring sharp white fangs. His eyes burned with a silent fury. Burned with a hungry fire as he stared at me.

I was too scared to move. Too frozen to break and run. Too numb in my fear to even think about grabbin' up a stick or rock. I only stood there. Frozen. Holding my breath.

Kitty's fierce growl, then his blood-chillin' shriek of pain, broke the silence.

It broke the spell which held my eyes to that hungry glare of the German shepherd.

I turned to see what was happening to my pup.

The four dogs had moved out into the open now. And the first one, the biggest of the pack, was locked in mortal combat with Kitty.

They growled and yelped. Tangled together in a

swirling mass of snapping jaws and bared fangs. Lea-pin' into the air, slashing and tearin' at each other with savage fury.

A movement on my left startled me.

The big German shepherd came loping across the clearing toward the terrifying fight.

I felt trembles start in the small of my back.

Then, like a branch snapping in a windstorm, somethin' in me snapped.

The old panic took hold of me. Shook me one time, real good, and sent me screamin' in a blind run to-ward the path.

It was like the day Sammy sicked his dog on me. Like the day when I was real little and that dog jumped on me near our apartment in St. Louis. Took me back to that hospital room where the nurses and doctors had to hold me down 'cause those rabies shots hurt so much I had to scream and jump until I was worn out.

All that came to me. Everything, all piled up to-gether. All the thoughts, memories, pain, fear. It all came tumbling through my head.

I screamed, but I didn't know the sound came from me. It sounded far off, like somebody else. The tears rolled down my cheeks.

And I ran. Ran like I'd never run before.

Chapter 12

It must have been a rock. Either that or a stick or a half-buried tree root. Whatever . . .

I remember somethin' hittin' the top of my boot, right about the ankle. Then I found myself flyin' through the air.

The thick brush snapped as I fell into it. Sharp branches stung against my half-frozen ears. Tore at the skin on my cheeks and face.

I hit with a bone-jarring thud that rattled my teeth. Knocked the breath clean out of me in one big whoosh.

A sharp pain bit into my knee. And when I finally

stopped tumbling and rolling, another sharp pain was jabbin' at my back.

The hurtin' must have been what snapped me out of my blind panic.

I sat up, gasping to catch my breath.

I felt my forehead wrinkle when I rubbed at my right knee. There was a tear in my pants. The damp, warm feel of blood around the tender flesh.

With a grunt, I raised up off the rock that was pokin' me in the back. Panted for air and looked around.

For a second, I couldn't remember where I was. It was like that day at the stadium playing football with the guys. Then the terror grabbed hold of me. I sorta blacked out for a second and didn't really remember what had happened.

Then I heard Kitty.

I don't know how I knew it was him. There were voices from other dogs. Growling. Snarlin' and barkin'. But when I heard Kitty's voice, I knew it was him.

He was still squallin' mad with fight. Growlin' and squealin' just like he had the day he tore into the cats.

Only this time the sound of him was somehow different.

Something that told he was in a fight to the death. Not a fight for food or for fun—a fight for his very life.

My legs held me when I stood. The right knee hurt somethin' terrible, but even limpin' bad, it didn't slow me much.

I had a stick in my hand. A big, heavy stick.

I don't remember hunting for it. Don't even remember picking it up. It was just there.

I reckon I could have been thinking a lot of things. Thinking about how I'd raised Kitty from a pup. How I'd kept him from starving to death. Remembering all the times we'd played together or chased around the countryside with Beauty. I could have been thinking that Kitty was trying to save our cow and her calf, and I should have been there helping him, instead of running off scared.

Only I didn't think any of those things. Not until after it was all over.

It was like my head was empty. I wasn't thinking anything at all.

I was running back up the path. Limping on my hurt knee and hanging onto the club in my hand for dear life.

Kitty's cry came to my ears again.

At that moment, his voice was the only thing in the world. Nothing else. No thoughts. No panic or fear of dogs. No feelin' of the darkness closing in around me. Just his voice. His hurt, desperate voice, growing weaker by the second.

A limping run broke me from the brushy path and into the clearing by the pond.

Across from me, I could see the dogs. Three of the five had jumped Kitty.

I could see him struggling, right square in the middle of them. Snarling and flinging himself, almost helpless as they dragged him to the ground.

The big German shepherd that had stared at me had hold of Kitty's leg. He stretched it out from him. Pulled him off balance just enough so the other two could knock him down.

One of the others had Kitty by one ear. But Kitty had him by the throat. Hanging to him, even while the other two dogs were rippin' him apart. Hanging to him with a death grip.

The third dog had Kitty by the back. Even in the half darkness of the little valley, I could see the blood shooting from beneath his fierce jaws.

The sight of those dogs trying to tear Kitty to shreds sent a fire boiling through me. My teeth clamped together so hard I could feel the grinding clean to the top of my head.

I raised the club with both hands.

Kitty cried out in pain. Even with his jaws clamped tight around the dog's throat, I could hear his whimpering voice telling the whole world he'd lost his battle.

I brought the club down with every ounce of strength in my body. It whistled through the crisp winter air. Found its mark, square in the center of the German shepherd's back.

He let out a startled yelp. I felt something crack.

Then, his legs flew out from under him. He fell to the ground with his mouth opening and closing. His legs churned every which way, but he couldn't get up.

I knew I'd broken his back.

The dog that had been biting Kitty's back had moved around in front of him. He had him by the soft part of the belly. I could see by his jaws the place where he'd torn a wide gap in Kitty's stomach.

He saw me, too. Just as I raised the club, he let go of Kitty and turned to run.

I brought the club down fast. Aimed blind and swung hard.

The blow caught him. It was a glancing blow. It struck against the side of his head. Then the end of my club broke as it slammed against the ground.

The dog yelped with pain. He staggered sideways, then fell to the ground. After wallering around for a second, he was on his feet. Yelping and pitching as he staggered in circles.

I knew I'd only dazed him, so I raised what was left of my club and started for him again.

I was so busy thinking about knocking those dogs off Kitty, I forgot about the two who were watching from the edge of the battle.

All at once, something hit the back of my leg. I felt a sharp, searing pain. Yelled out. Screamed as long, white fangs tore through my flesh and into muscle.

I felt myself falling.

I screamed again.

Suddenly, Kitty came to life.

For a time there, I thought he was almost dead. His stomach was torn open and there were bleeding cuts all over his back and shoulders. He was so weak that he could just barely hold to that other dog's throat.

But just as I hit the ground, I saw him let go of his death grip and charge toward me.

His attack knocked the dog from my leg. I felt the flesh tear between his teeth. Heard the ripping sound of my pant leg shredding away.

Kitty roared and snarled with more fury and anger than I ever heard. He was like the swirling wind from a bad storm. His rage knocked the dog loose from me and sent them both spinning toward the center of the dry pond.

I lay there, watching Kitty take the dog away from me. Then my startled mind cleared enough to remember that there were still two more dogs.

Trembling, I staggered to my feet. Any second, I

expected another dog to come tearing into me. Expected to feel the pain of fierce teeth.

They weren't there.

The other dog that had been watching the fight and the one I'd hit with the glancing blow against the side of the head were gone. Scared and shaking, I looked all around for them. Far up the hill I could hear them moving through the brush at a fast run.

The German shepherd I'd hit lay still and lifeless on the ground. The dog Kitty had by the throat was staggering around a few feet from me. His head hung low, and I could hear the bubbling sound when he tried to breathe.

I stared into the darkness at him. Blood dripped from his mouth. In his throat, where Kitty's jaws had been, blood and air bubbled out from deep holes.

He staggered some. Fell. His throat rattled for breath as he died.

All at once, the chills shot up my back. I didn't know what it was at first. Then I noticed the quiet.

Only a second ago, Kitty's battle had been raging behind me.

Now there was nothing there but quiet.

I wheeled around.

Kitty was laying on his back. The other dog stood over him. His teeth were buried in Kitty's neck.

"No!" I screamed.

I raced toward them. Planted one foot just as I got there and kicked with the other.

The dog yelped. I felt the toe of my boot dig deep into his ribs. He let go of Kitty's throat and took off running. A few feet away, he stopped. I grabbed up a stick and took after him. Tail tucked, he lit out for good.

I guess he had been so busy fighting, he forgot all about the cow and calf he and the other dogs in the pack had come after in the first place. 'Cause, when he turned to run, he went straight up the draw where the heifer and her baby were.

It was so dark in that draw, I never did see what happened. A few minutes after the dog ran in there, though, I heard the old cow bellow. Then I heard the dog yelp and a whole bunch of brush snapping and crashing around.

I knew the old heifer took care of him, but good.

The battle was over. I turned on shaking legs and went back to where I'd left my dog lying in the bottom of the dry pond bed.

I knew he'd be dead when I got there. Dead, or so far gone I couldn't help him. But I had to know for sure.

The tears rolled down my cheeks. I wiped them with my coat sleeve and knelt beside my dog.

He whimpered when I touched him.

"You're gonna be all right, boy," I said.

Only I knew I was lying. I knew he was gonna die.

Then, my mouth fell so wide open it nearly touched the ground.

Somehow, Kitty was on his feet.

He was wagging that long, floppy tail. Bouncing around and lopping me in the face with his sloppy, wet tongue.

I didn't push him away like I usually did. I just let him lick me. I held him in my arms and cried. Laughed and cried till I could hardly catch my breath.

"You're gonna be all right, boy," I said again.

This time, I wasn't lying to him. That thick hide of his had saved him from the dog's neck hold.

I calmed him some. Held him out at arm's length to have a good look at him.

There were cuts all over his back and shoulders. One ear was bit clean off—nothing left but a short, bloody stub. The tear in his stomach was the worst.

But none of his insides had spilled out. And I knew that if I could get to the house where Mama could take care of him, he'd be good as new in no time.

"All I got to do is get you home," I said.

Then I repeated the words, like they were far off and frightening, "All I got to do is get you home."

But how?

Home was two miles away. Two miles of hard walking. I was afraid to let Kitty walk, 'cause he might tear that stomach wound open and really hurt himself.

I wasn't in much shape to carry him, either. One leg was pretty well torn up. First from bustin' my knee open when I fell on that sharp rock, and second from having the back of it chewed by the dog.

While Kitty and me were fighting for our lives, I hadn't noticed it. Now that everything was over and I'd sat down to rest, I could feel the pain. It was an aching, throbbing pain. Hurting bad enough to bring the tears to my eyes.

The little valley where our dry pond sat was dark now. There was a gray glow in the sky. The sun had set beyond the horizon and the light from the edges of high clouds was all we had. It wasn't enough to see by.

I sat down beside Kitty. He crawled up against me and whined. When I petted him, he licked my hand.

That's when it started coming to me, all the things that had happened, all the things that could have happened.

It gave me the shakes, all over. I felt sick to my stomach, too. Kitty nuzzled up against me. Licked at me, like he was trying to take care of me. And all along, he was the one needing care.

That made me cry even more.

I felt so helpless. I was hurt and the cold was moving into me. Coming with the night to chill my already aching body. Thoughts and visions of the bad things that could have happened to me and Kitty kept coming to my mind. Worst of all, my pup needed help and there was no way I could get it for him.

That's when I heard the horn honking.

The sound came from the pickup down in the muddy field.

I threw my head back and started yelling.

Mama was there. There, probably worried sick about me and trying to find me. I hollered louder. Kept hollering until I saw the flashlight bobbing and flickering up the path toward the pond.

That flashlight was the prettiest sight I ever saw.

Chapter 13

I was right proud of Mama. She didn't make a big fuss and go to bawlin' when she found us. She didn't get gushy and smooch all over me after she got us back to the house, either.

She kept her head real good. There was so much that needed to be done, I reckon she didn't have time. She got things done, too, without the least little fuss.

First off, she tried to call a doctor for me. It was late, and all she got were those recording things on the phone that told her to leave her name and number and the doctor would call in the morning. So she called Brad's mother, her closest friend, and she said she knew a doctor, and they'd be there quick as possible.

Next, Mama called the vet. She told me she didn't know a thing about patching up a dog. And after I kept pestering her for a while, she called.

Mr. Stubble got there before the doctor did. He told Mama he'd called the Sheriff, and they'd come and find the dogs. Take them to Oklahoma City for the tests to make sure they didn't have rabies.

That sent a scare running through me. I could still remember having to take those rabies shots back in St. Louis. I prayed and begged that I wouldn't have to go through that pain again.

After that, he set to work patching Kitty up. He said the cuts and bites weren't bad, but that the one in his stomach and another on the back of his neck would need stitches.

Kitty was brave about fighting off a pack of wild dogs to save the little calf. But when it came to being doctored, I reckon he was an even bigger coward than I was.

Mr. Stubble got out a couple of shots to give him, and Kitty threw a regular fit. He started squalling and finally broke away from Mama and took out running.

I bet Mama and the vet chased that crazy dog through the house for thirty minutes before they finally caught him and wrestled him to the kitchen table.

The shots calmed him. But not enough to keep him from yowling and snapping when the vet tried to stitch up his wounds.

It took Mama and me and the vet to hold that dog down.

Brad and his mom got there with the doctor about the time we were halfway through. Brad and his mom took our places holding Kitty down while the doctor fixed me up.

I was sure glad when he said there wasn't any need for stitches. He gave me three shots. Cleaned out the cut in my knee with hydrogen peroxide and then put a butterfly bandage over it. He sprayed the dog bite with some kind of disinfectant that almost made me climb the wall. Then he said there wasn't much else he could do for it.

The Sheriff and a bunch of men drove up about ten minutes later. I told them where the dogs had jumped Kitty and me, and a whole bunch of men started out to find them.

One of the men told Mama he had called the state health department in Oklahoma City, and they said they'd have men waiting there to examine the dogs for rabies as soon as they brought them in.

The vet said there probably wasn't much need to

worry about rabies, 'cause it was more likely in spring than winter, like now.

That didn't help me, though. There was a knot in my stomach. A shaking in my arms that just wouldn't stop when I thought about those rabies shots.

After a little bit, I started feeling sleepy, though. Mama told me it was one of the shots the doctor gave me.

I fought it as long as I could. There was too much going on for me to sleep. Too many people around. Too much commotion.

But fighting was no use. Whatever was in that shot was stronger than I was and, in no time, I felt my eyes gettin' droopy and my head rolling around. I finally gave it up. Went to sleep despite the noise and commotion.

The sound of a siren brought my eyes open. I could tell by the light coming in the window that it was daytime.

The siren got louder and louder. Then I could tell it was right outside the house and still going.

I blinked a couple of times. Sat up on the edge of the couch and looked around.

Our living room was filled with people. The vet and the doctor were still there. So were Brad and his mom. Sometime while I was asleep, Brad's father had come. There were neighbor folks, too. The Jessens from about a mile north of our place. The Rodgers and the Simmons and the Priddles were there, too.

Everybody was watching the door.

The door flew open and a man who had come with the Sheriff last night rushed in. He was waving a piece of paper in his hand. Smiling from ear to ear.

"They're all right," he shouted. "The dogs are okay. No rabies."

What he said sent a chill through me. Made my heart pound till I thought it was gonna jump right out of my chest.

All the people sitting around cheered. Then, everybody looked at me.

All the folks made over me. Patted me on the back and shoulder while Mama hugged me up tight.

"Did you hear?" Mama sniffed.

I hugged her.

"Yes, Mama. I heard."

Everybody was laughing and talking. And suddenly, above all the commotion, I heard Dad's voice.

"What the . . ." He stopped. Cleared his throat. "What on earth's happened?"

Dad liked to throw a wall-eyed fit. He kept running around the house asking questions, yellin', and, in general, making a complete pest out of himself.

I didn't blame him for getting so excited. After all,

there was a sheriff's car with its siren going outside. Then there were a whole bunch of other cars, not to mention all the people inside the house.

I reckon he would have gone right on asking Mama what had happened—then running off to ask somebody else, before she could answer him—if it hadn't been for Mr. Stubble.

The vet finally told Dad he was gonna give him one of the tranquilizer shots he used on cows if he didn't settle down.

Mama told Dad all that had gone on. And everybody else in the house had to jump in and add to her story. The men from the Sheriff's department kept saying how brave I was and how they'd hate to tangle with me and my dog, after what we'd done to those three hounds. The doctor told him how brave I was about getting doctored. And the vet told him how Kitty had acted, and about him and Mama having to chase him all over the house.

Everybody was excited and happy. Everybody was laughing and all trying to talk at once.

It was pretty exciting for me, too. But after listening to all that stuff for well over an hour, I got kinda bored with it.

Everybody was clumped up around Mama and Dad at the kitchen table. And since nobody was watching, I figured this would be as good a time as any for Brad and me to sneak off.

Mama and Dad had been saying I could have Brad out to spend the night. But what with all the chores and school and Dad being away, we never had time.

While everybody was busy talking to Dad, I motioned Brad over. He had me put my arm over his shoulder so he could help me walk. Then we headed upstairs.

Mama had put Kitty on a pile of towels at the foot of my bed. He was still kinda weak and groggy. Instead of waggling all over and trying to jump up on me when I came in, he just lifted his head a little and whimpered.

Brad and I sat down beside him and petted him.

"Even all chewed up and with stitches in him, he's still a fine-lookin' dog," Brad said.

I shrugged.

"He's just an ole stray. Not worth much. He's sorta like a bad cold. He came along one day, and I haven't been able to get rid of him."

I was only teasing about the way I felt toward Kitty. He knew it, too, 'cause his tail kept wagging all the time I was talking about him.

Sure, in the beginning, it was like I said. I didn't think much of him. I didn't want him around.

Now it was different.

I never thought I could stand being around dogs,

much less love one. But I loved Kitty. Loved him more than just about anything.

That's why, when he died, something died in me, too.

Chapter 14

Kitty and me were regular heroes for a long time. The newspaper in town wrote up a big story about how the two of us destroyed the pack of wild dogs that had been killing calves out west of Chickasha.

Our wounds healed quickly, and it was no time before we were out riding the country again. Opening neighbor's gates and exploring all over.

An oil company moved in down the road. They put up a tall derrick and started drilling. I spent a big part of the summer watching them and visiting with some of the men at the oil well.

A fella named Arthur Sendens took a real liking to me and Kitty. He used to share his lunch with us. And

I reckon he told me everything there was to know about drilling for oil and operating an oil well. He even took me up on top of the derrick once.

We were headed over to visit Arthur one Friday afternoon. Mom had let me invite Brad out to spend a few days, and I was gonna ask Arthur if it was all right to bring him to see the rig. I was also hoping he would let me and Brad ride to the top of the derrick with him.

Beauty and I came up at a gallop. Right as we got in sight of the rig, I could see Arthur. He was standing on the boom, way up top of the rig.

He was waving his arms. And above the sound of the machines, I could hear him yelling, "Wait! Stop!"

I yanked Beauty up. Yelled for Kitty. Only, Kitty was thinking about his stomach, like usual, and expecting Arthur to feed him when he got to the oil well.

I yelled again, but Kitty never heard me.

There was a big truck backed up to the rig with a load of pipe on it.

Kitty went tearing past the side of it. Just as he did, they released the load of drilling pipe. Arthur was yelling at the men, trying to stop them.

But they didn't hear him.

The pipes rolled and tumbled off the truck.

Kitty was right under them.

He never heard those heavy, crushing pipes coming down on him. Never heard me or Arthur yelling for him to run.

The men were real sorry it had happened. They must have told me that a hundred times while everybody was working to move the pile of pipes.

Arthur picked up Kitty's body after the men had moved everything. He turned around, trying to hide the sight from me.

"I'm sorry, Ricky," he said. "I'll take care of him for you."

I swallowed down my cries.

"Is he dead?"

I didn't need to ask. I already knew my pup was gone.

"Yes," Arthur answered.

I swallowed again.

"I better take him home," I said. "He was my dog. I need to take my dog home."

I carried him on my lap, across the saddle. Beauty moved at a slow walk. Her sleepy head drooped low.

I couldn't help thinking about all the bad things I'd said to Kitty. About how I kept telling him I was gonna bash his head with a rock when I first found him. About how I kept telling him I was gonna run him off as soon as he got well enough to walk. About how I'd called him a coward the day he got the cow to chase me.

Now, he was gone. Now it was too late to tell him that I never meant all those things. Too late to tell him how much I loved him. Needed him.

I reckon he knew, though. I guess he knew that all along.

I don't remember crying much. Or feeling sick to my stomach or setting up a big fuss when I told Mama and Dad.

I just felt empty inside.

I buried him on top of the terrace by the barn. That was his favorite spot. The place he used to sit and soak up the sun while he was watching for the cats.

Then I put Beauty in her pen and went to the house.

Mama and Dad tried to talk to me. Tried to help me feel better. I listened to all they had to say. Listened when Dad told me I had to remember the good things, the fun things, me and Kitty used to do together. And that how dying was natural and how if it hadn't been for that accident, Kitty would have died sooner or later, 'cause dying was just a part of living.

I listened to them, but it didn't help. That empty feeling stayed inside me. Stayed there, making me wake up at night. Making me eat only half the food on my plate. Making the corners of my mouth droop instead of smiling.

Kitty was dead. I knew I'd never get over the empty feeling inside me.

Dad wanted to get me a dog. But I told him I didn't want one. I guess he understood, 'cause after I told him that, he never mentioned it again.

Mama tried to cheer me up, too. She took me swimming and visiting with friends in town. She even let Brad come out after a couple of weeks and spend four days with us.

Only, nothing seemed to help.

I didn't mope around or not eat. Somehow, I'd managed to hide the way I felt. Managed to smile so Mama and Dad wouldn't worry about me so.

But inside, I still felt the same. Still sad and lonely.

The week before school started, Mama threw me a real big birthday party. She invited all my friends, and she found out from school who was gonna be in my homeroom in sixth grade and invited most of them, too.

I don't guess Mama knew how I felt about Sammy Darlinger, 'cause she invited him.

Sammy brought his dog. When I saw it, I ran to tell him that I didn't want that stinking dog of his here and for his mama to take it back home. But Sammy's mama just dropped him out of the car. And before I could get there, she drove off.

It was a pretty good party. I managed to laugh and play with the guys. But all the time, inside, I was wishing it was over so I could be alone.

We played cowboys and Indians on the rock hill. I let some of them ride Beauty with me. Then we went back to the house for cake and ice cream.

Mama and Dad had saved their present till last. It was a football. I'd always wanted a football, and I tried to let them know how happy it made me.

We chose up teams. I was one captain and Brad was the other. We played in the pasture out south of the barn. It was about the only flat place on our land, except for the stuff Dad had planted in next year's wheat.

As usual, Sammy was his hateful self. Joel Havely was the littlest kid at my party. So it only stood to reason that Sammy would single him out to pick on.

A couple of times, Sammy tackled Joel real hard. Then, he tackled him one time when he didn't even have the ball. Joel got hurt and started crying.

Since he was on Brad's team, Brad tried to straighten him up. Sammy didn't listen. Since it was my party, I figured it was up to me to say something.

"Why don't you leave Joel alone, Sammy?"

He got that real smart look on his face.

"Mind your own business," he snapped. "I ain't hurtin' him none. He's just being a baby."

"You're being too rough, Sammy. Why don't you leave him alone?"

Sammy put his hands on his hips. Marched up to me when I helped Joel off the ground and dusted his shirt.

"You gonna make me, Ricky?"

I looked him square in the eye.

"If I have to. And I know better than to turn my back on you like last time."

"You touch me," he threatened. "You hit me, I'll sick my dog on you."

I stopped. Stared at him.

All of a sudden, there was a big commotion over by the barn.

Growling and barking and all sorts of racket.

We forgot the argument and went racing around to see what was going on. Sammy's dog was standing over a little pup. He had him pinned down with his front paws, biting at him.

The pup was so little and scrawny he didn't stand a chance. From the looks of him, he was probably a stray that somebody had dumped. Wherever he came from, he had gone without food for a long time and wasn't in any shape to put up a fight against the bigger dog.

"Call your dog off," Brad yelled.

Sammy came rushing up beside him.

"Get him, Butch. Tear him up, boy. That Butch is a great fighter. He never has lost a fight."

Everybody was jumping around, yelling at the two dogs.

I still don't know what made me do it. But for some reason, without thinking, I ran over to them. I grabbed Sammy's dog by the scruff of the neck and the tail. Picked him up and slung him. He flapped against the barn with a thud. Then stood there on the ground shaking his head.

Sammy ran up and grabbed me.

"You leave my dog alone," he yelled. "I'll pound your head in if you ever do my dog like that again."

I'd had just about enough of Sammy, too.

I felt my fist draw up at my side. I don't remember hitting him. But afterwards, my hand hurt. And when Sammy straightened up, there was blood dripping from his nose.

"Sick him, Butch," Sammy cried. "Get him, boy."

Butch was about as snotty as Sammy. When he called, Butch came growling and bouncing around. He was a little confused about who he was supposed to sick, though.

By the time Sammy convinced him it was me he was supposed to be chasing, it was too late. I'd grabbed up a stick and was waiting for him.

When Butch saw that stick, he turned tail and lit out around the barn, whining. I threw the stick down and whirled on Sammy.

"You want a black eye to go along with your bloody nose?" I asked him.

Sammy took out, crying, for the house.

All the guys laughed. Then, they started petting and making over the stray pup that Sammy's dog had beat up.

"You guys leave him alone," I told them after a minute or so. "Let's go finish our game."

Everybody wanted to know why. So I told them that if we petted and fed stray dogs, they'd stick around. If they left him alone, he'd finally go on and find someplace else to live.

"But you need a dog," Brad argued. "Why don't you keep this one?"

"I don't want a dog," I snapped. "Now come on."

We went back to our game. After a while, everybody's mom came and took them home. I hadn't had to help Dad with the chores today 'cause it was my birthday. So I was sittin' in the kitchen polishing off the last of the birthday cake when Mama went to feed the cats.

I hadn't given another thought to the pup up by the barn. I meant what I'd said to the guys. "I don't want another dog. If we don't pet or feed him, he'll leave."

I guess not thinking about a dog was what surprised me so much when I heard him barking outside.

All of a sudden, I heard Mama scream. Then there was a commotion like you never heard before.

Squalling and hissing. Barking and growling.

I jumped up and ran for the back door.

When I got there, I saw that crazy pup tangled up with our cats. They were fuzzed up mad and determined to fight him off their food.

Mama was square in the middle of things. Jumping from one foot to the other and yelling.

It didn't take long for the cats to lick him good. One was balled up on his back, clawing and biting. Tufts of hair were flying every which way.

The pup gave the fight to them and lit out for the barn. He had his tail tucked and was yelping and squalling all the way. Setting up so much of a fuss you woulda thought our cats were still chasing him.

That's when I heard myself laughing.

It was a real laugh this time. Not a put-on laugh to keep Mama and Dad from worrying. A real laugh that came from way down deep in my stomach.

I watched that little, scraggly pup run for the barn. Laughed and laughed until the tears came to my eyes.

When I was all laughed and all cried out, I went to the refrigerator and got out some meat scraps and a bowl of milk.

I knew just what I was gonna say to him when I got to the barn, too.

I'd say, "You stinking, no-good pup. I'll feed you. Not 'cause I like you, but 'cause I don't want you starving to death. But, soon as you're well enough, I'm gonna run your tail off. You understand?"

That's what I'd tell him. I'd tell him, but I knew he wouldn't really believe me.